# INDIGO NIGHTMARES

(Colors of Evil, Book 3)

## By Cynthia Hickey

ISBN: 978-1-0882-1464-0

# DEDICATION

To those who kept asking for the series to be finished. This book is for you.

# Chapter 1

"We're blood." Devonne Williams leaned across the small kitchen table and stared into the scared face of the boy in front of him. "You hear me, nephew?"

Kamal nodded. "I hear you, but I said I won't join you."

Devonne narrowed his eyes and sat back in his chair. "Oh, I think you will." He grinned. "I've seen how much you care for your family, especially your little brother. What's his name? Lincoln, right?"

"You leave him out of this." A trickle of dread skittered down Kamal's spine. Would his uncle really hurt one of his own to get Kamal to join his gang? "What is so important that you would harm your own blood? With my father in jail, I'm the man of the house. I can't be running off doing what you want. I've got responsibilities."

"What's important is the fact I say so." Devonne steepled his fingers under his dark chin. "You can provide for your family easier and make more money dealing for me."

"I don't want that kind of money." Kamal stormed from the apartment and down the stairs. Outside, he took a deep breath and closed his eyes.

This wasn't the first time his uncle had threatened his family. He meant business, which meant Kamal needed help. As if drawn by a magnet, he turned and headed to the center of town and stopped in front of the red brick building that housed Upton Falls's police department. If his uncle found out what he considered doing, he'd kill Kamal and his family.

"Can I help you, son?" A tall man in cowboy boots stepped out of the glass doors. "You look as if you've got a lot on your mind."

Kamal recognized the new chief-of-police from his picture in the newspaper last year. He swallowed against the mountain in his throat. "Uh, no, just walking."

The man cocked his head. "You sure? I don't bite." He smiled.

"Yeah, I'm sure." Kamal shoved his hands into his pockets and hurried away. He needed to really think this through. If he decided to snitch, there would be no turning back. Consequences would be severe.

Lincoln sat on the cracked stoop of their rundown house when Kamal got home. He scratched in the dirt with a stick.

Kamal sat next to his eight-year-old sibling. "What's up bro? You look down."

"Mom's drunk again, and I'm hungry."

Kamal sighed and put his arm around his brother. "Come on. I'll fix you something." There had better be food in the house.

Nothing but a swallow of milk and crumbs in the bottom

of a cereal box. Kamal handed what little they had to Lincoln, then marched to the living room where his mother lay sprawled across the sofa. "Where's the food stamp card?" He shook her awake.

"Purse," she slurred, not opening her eyes. "Don't take them all. I'm going to sell some."

No, she wasn't. Kamal fished her card from her wallet and took Lincoln's hand. "We're buying enough food for the month, buddy." If, and it was a big if, there was any leftover then their mother could sell what was left.

At the store on the corner, Kamal filled a shopping cart with all the items he could get with WIC for free, then started on other things. Mom could get her liquor money somewhere else.

"When Dad gets out of prison, we'll never be hungry." Lincoln hung a six-pack of lemon-lime soda on the cart.

"We can always hope." He paid for the groceries and pushed the cart home. He'd return it the next day. Once the groceries were put away, he made Lincoln a peanut butter and jelly sandwich. He glanced around the dirty room.

The sink overflowed with dishes. His mother's drunken snores drifted from the living room. If Kamal joined his uncle's gang, they could get out of that dump, find someplace nicer.

He looked back at Lincoln. No, he couldn't subject his brother to the gang lifestyle. He patted his brother's head. "Stay home. I'll be back soon." He was going to do what he had almost done earlier.

Again, he stopped at the steps. Once he walked through those doors, there would be no turning back. He squared his shoulders and pushed open the door. "I need to see a cop."

~

Aislinn McFarland turned away from the front desk. "I'm Detective McFarland. How may I help you?" The African-American teen looked as if the word boo would scare him right out the door. "Why don't you come to my office? The receptionist will get you a soda."

"Dr. Pepper."

"All right." Linn chuckled and motioned her head. "Come on."

She led him to the smallest conference room and motioned for him to have a seat. She took the seat next to him. "How about you start with your name, then tell me why you're here." She slid a sheet of paper across to him. "Address too, please."

He scratched his head. "I'm Kamal Williams. My uncle is Devonne Williams. I want to help you put him behind bars so he'll leave my family alone." He wrote down the requested information, then slid the paper back.

She hadn't been expecting that. "Devonne Williams as in the gang leader?"

"Yeah." Kamal lowered his dark eyes. "I'm willing to be a snitch."

"How old are you?"

"Sixteen." He raised his head and met her gaze. "I know there's a law that says you can use anyone over the age of thirteen."

"Yes, with the approval of a judge." Linn straightened in her seat and studied the handsome young man in front of her. Everything in her refused to use an underage informant. It wasn't ethical in her book, and there was no way she wanted to risk the life of a child. "Why do you want to do this? It's incredibly dangerous. You could lose your life."

"I could lose my life without helping you. I got a better chance with you." Stubbornness crossed his face.

Linn folded her arms and leaned on the table. "Why don't you just tell me what you know and go home? We don't need to use you in that way."

"No. This is the only way to get close to him." He frowned. "You're a cop. You're supposed to help people."

"I'm helping you by saying no."

Kamal leaped to his feet. "You're sentencing people to death by saying no." He turned and dashed down the hall. By the time Linn followed, he was out the door.

"What's up?" Drew came out of his office. "That boy was here earlier, but stood outside."

"Getting up the nerve to come in, I guess." She brushed past him into the room and closed the door. "His name is Kamal Williams. He says he's Devonne Williams's nephew."

"What in the hell did he come here for?" Drew sat behind his desk.

"He wants us to use him as an informant to put his uncle away." Linn shook her head and perched on the corner of his desk. "I told him no."

Drew's blue eyes widened. "That's good."

"What? You don't sound convinced." She shook her foot in agitation.

"No, I agree. It's only…" he ran his hand through his dark blond hair. "It would be nice to bring that man down."

"Not by using a child."

"Absolutely. But that young man might be able to give us the name of someone older willing to help."

Linn shrugged. "It's worth a try." She leaned forward and kissed him. "I'll get Steve and pay a visit to his home."

He clutched the front of her blouse and pulled her down for another kiss. This one lingered, causing a heat to rise up her neck and into her face. "Think on that while you're pounding the pavement," he whispered against her lips.

She chuckled. "As if I could forget." She fanned her face, tossed him a smile over her shoulder, and left his office.

Steve glanced up from his desk when she entered the office they shared. His yellow-green eyes focused on her face. "Are you coming down with something? You're flushed."

"Nope." She should have splashed cold water on her face. "Want to go visit a kid in the ghetto?"

"Okay. Why?" He grabbed his jacket from the back of his chair.

As they made their way to her car, she told him of Kamal's visit. "Drew and I are hoping there's an adult in the house as willing to help us as the boy is."

He shrugged. "We might get lucky."

Fifteen minutes later, Linn parked in front of a white house badly in need of paint. What yard there was held nothing more than dirt and trampled weeds. A child's bicycle with a flat tire leaned against the wall. Her heart always broke when she saw the conditions in which some children grew up. She knocked on the door.

A little boy with mocha-colored skin answered. "Are you social services? Because my mother said any time a white person comes to the door I gotta ask."

Linn smiled. "No, we're detectives. Is Kamal here?"

The boy's features hardened. "I won't let you lock my

brother up. He didn't do nothing."

Linn bent to look into his eyes. "You're right. I only need to ask him a question."

"He ain't here."

"Is your mom or dad here?"

"Dad's locked up, and Mom is passed out."

Linn straightened and met Steve's stern gaze. "Will you let your brother know we stopped by?" Linn handed the boy her business card. "Tell him to give me a call."

"Okay." He slammed the door.

"Do we need to get social services out here?" Steve asked.

"The boy looked fine. No visible signs of abuse. I'll come back in a few days. If anything concerns me after I get inside, I'll make the call." She stood on the sidewalk and stared up and down the street.

Unfriendly glares from nearby residents told her that she and Steve were not wanted there. She sighed and got back in the car. It wouldn't do Kamal any good for his neighbors to grow suspicious. Even though they had agreed not to use him to get close to his uncle, the neighbors didn't know that and could cause serious problems for the young man.

Problems that could result in his death.

# Chapter 2

Kamal sent multiple glances over his shoulder the next morning as he walked Lincoln to the bus stop. He didn't want to believe Uncle Devonne would make good on his threat. They were his blood. Still, Mom said the man had no conscience.

He bent and peered into his little brother's face. "You be good. Stay close to your friends. Don't wander off alone. I'll be here to get you when you come home."

"What's wrong?" Lincoln frowned and clutched his backpack.

"Nothing. Go on. The bus won't wait forever." Kamal waited until Lincoln was safely seated and the bus door closed before heading to his job at the grocery store. The job that kept the utilities on in their low-income housing.

When had Kamal become the main provider? When Dad got arrested and Mom started drinking, that's when. He kicked a soda can into the gutter. All of Kamal's problems could be traced back to Devonne.

He slammed through the back door of the store. Why wouldn't the cops help him? Weren't they there to serve and protect?

"Who got up in your grill?" Leroy, the other stocker for the store, threw a roll of paper towels at Kamal's head.

"Cops."

The other guy cursed. "They'll do that man. They should all be dead."

"And let each man fend for themselves?" Kamal shrugged and pushed a cart of boxes out of the aisle. "A lot of people wouldn't make it."

"Survival of the fittest, dude."

Kamal shook his head. He didn't believe that way. Who would look out for the women and children? If he believed as Leroy did, Lincoln would be on his own. Maybe Kamal needed to pay another visit to that female cop. He stuck his hand in his pocket and fingered the business card Lincoln had given him.

Her showing up at the house showed promise.

~

"I just can't get that boy out of my mind." Linn pulled on a pair of black pants.

"What boy?" Drew met her gaze through the bedroom mirror.

"Kamal. After visiting his house yesterday, I really feel he's crying out for help." She grabbed a light blue blouse off the bed. "Not just with his uncle, but with his family."

"Gang members don't usually want us meddling in their family affairs." Drew turned and moved her hands aside, taking over the buttoning of her blouse. "How do you feel about being late for work today?"

She ran her fingers over the scars on his chest, a daily reminder of the explosion that had killed him. Steve's quick thinking and CPR training had brought Drew back to her. She wrapped her arms around his neck. "I know you're the boss and all, but we can't leave everything to a skeleton crew." She kissed him and slipped from his arms. "Get dressed, handsome. I'll make the coffee."

Every day she could keep Drew in his office was a good day. She'd handled things without him before, she could do so again. If something were to happen to him—she shrugged off the melancholy feeling and measured coffee grounds into the pot.

"You're worrying again." Drew leaned against the kitchen door jamb. "I recognize the crease between your eyes."

"Just thinking."

He moved behind her, slipping his arms around her and resting his chin on her head. "I'm here, Linn. I don't plan on going anywhere."

"Sometimes life takes that plan away." She poured water into the maker. "I know we're law enforcement. I know that in my head. But in my heart, I'm your fiancé. A woman who worries every time her man straps on his gun and leaves the house."

"Now you know how I feel. Let's get married and get you pregnant." He turned her to face him, his eyes sparkling. "Then, you could stay home and care for our passel of kids."

She raised her eyebrows. "Passel of kids? Just how many do you want?"

"At least six."

She laughed. "I don't think I have enough time left to

give you six.”

“It sure would be fun trying.”

“Stop it.” She poured coffee into two travel mugs and handed him his. “You’re like a teenage boy today.”

“I’m like that every day when you’re around.”

By the time they reached the precinct, Linn had managed to push aside her fear for Drew’s safety, at least temporarily. She plopped in her office chair and propped her booted feet on her desk before riffling through her messages.

“I’m glad we don’t share a desk,” Steve said.

“My boots are clean.”

“Not clean enough. I think I see gum.”

“What?” She let her feet fall with a thud, then lifted them one at a time to inspect the bottom. “No, there isn’t.”

“That young man is here to see you again.” The receptionist’s voice came through the intercom.

“Put him in conference room one and get him a Dr. Pepper.” Linn stood. “Would you like to join me?”

“Sure.” Steve followed her to the conference room where a very nervous Kamal paced from one end of the small space to another.

“Sit down, please.” Linn motioned to a chair and closed the door before setting the can of soda on the table.

“I’m on break. I don’t have much time.” Kamal crossed his arms. “I heard you went to my crib.”

“Yes, you have an adorable little brother.” Linn leaned back in her seat. Cute, but rude, the little scamp.

“That’s why I want you to reconsider helping me.” He planted his hands flat on the tabletop. “Something bad will happen to him if you don’t.”

“Are you threatening me, young man?” She motioned

to Steve to keep his distance. From the look in his eyes, he wanted to throttle Kamal.

"No. Ugh." Kamal rolled his shoulders. "Someone will die as a lesson to me. I can't join my uncle's gang. I can't. That's not who I am."

"We'll put your family in protective custody."

"You aren't listening!" He slammed his hand on the table.

"Whoa." Drew entered the room and put his hands on Kamal's shoulders. "Relax, son. We're going to help you without having to use you as an informant. We can put an undercover—"

Kamal's eyes hardened. "That's the dumbest idea I've ever heard. Devonne will see right through that. He only uses family and close friends in his ranks, never a stranger."

Linn pressed her lips together. That did complicate things a bit. Ever since Devonne's gang had moved to Upton Falls two years ago, they'd wanted to bring him down. Now, the opportunity presented itself and the only way to get on the inside was to use a kid. She just couldn't bring herself to do so. From the look on Drew's face, he couldn't either.

"We'll keep a close eye on you and your family. I will not use a minor to get close to a killer. End of subject."

"You're all crazy!" Kamal punched the wall. "You'd better hope nothing happens to my family. My Dad knows people."

"That is definitely a threat." Drew narrowed his eyes. "I think you need to leave before I arrest you. Detective Chavez will escort you out. I think our new recruit is waiting," he told Steve. "You can bring her back when you return."

Steve nodded and grasped Kamal by the arm. "Let's go,

champ."

~

In the parking lot, the fight seemed to leave the boy. He hung his head. "Sorry, but y'all are making a big mistake." He shoved his hands in his pockets and shuffled down the sidewalk.

Steve wished they could help him, but what the boy asked was…well, he agreed with Linn. It was unethical. He'd heard of it happening in larger cities, but this was Upton Falls. A place where crime used to be almost nil until the gangs moved in.

Sighing, he entered the precinct and glanced around the waiting area until his gaze landed on a woman dressed in the dark blues of a cop. Her dark hair was pulled into a bun. Hazel eyes smiled at him as she stood and held out her hand.

"Lydia Gonzalez."

He returned the shake. "Detective Steve Chavez. The chief and my partner are waiting to meet you." He cleared his suddenly dry throat and led her to the conference room.

Linn perched on the edge of the table, blushing as they walked in. She laughed and hopped to the floor.

"Don't mind them," Steve said. "They're a couple who can't grasp proper work behavior."

Linn thrust out her hand. "Welcome to the nut house. I'm Detective Linn McFarland and this is Chief Andrew Wayne."

Lydia shook Linn's hand, then turned to the chief. "I'm excited to start working here. It's small enough to be the perfect first assignment."

Steve rolled his eyes. Once upon a time that had been a true statement. In the last two years, a gang moved in, his psycho twin brother left a trail of dead women who looked like Linn, and Queen Coral had kept, played with, and then killed several men, her sights on Steve before they took her down. The sleepy town had awakened with a vengeance. "You'll get broken in in no time."

Where were they going to put her? The one office he shared with Linn was already crowded to where a body couldn't move.

"We'll move a desk into your office," Wayne explained as if he'd read Steve's mind. "It'll fit with some rearranging."

Linn sighed and shook her head. "We'll be packed in like sardines. Come on Gonzalez. Let's get this party started."

"Why a new hire?" Steve asked.

Wayne shrugged. "We had money in the budget. Plus, this gives us someone who can pound the pavements, leaving the more serious crimes to you and Linn. It'll free up a lot of your investigating time. Her partner arrives later today."

"There's no way you'll fit two desks in the office."

"Construction starts tomorrow to expand the room." Wayne clapped him on the shoulder. "Lighten up, Chavez. Haven't you learned by now that I have an answer to everything?"

Sometimes it was hard for Steve to like the man who had stolen his heart's desire. That moment was one of those times. Once upon a time he'd hoped to win over Linn. "I'll go help the women." He marched to the office where Linn and Gonzalez chattered like old friends as they shoved desks against walls.

Steve hated facing the brick wall. "Turn the desks to

face the center of the room. We need room for people to sit when we talk to them." He turned his desk around, leaving him just enough room to slide a chair in and open the drawers.

When they'd finished, the small office had a cleared space in the center of the room that allowed them to each have a chair in front of their desk as well as behind. "We'll be able to hear every word of each others' conversations," he said.

"Only until they build on. In a month's time, we'll have plenty of space."

"Where is Gonzalez's partner going to sit?"

"In the corner for now." Linn flashed a grin. "I'll leave you two to get acquainted while I get the files from Lucy."

Incompetent receptionist. She'd worked for them since shortly after the Queen Coral case and took forever to do simple filing. She'd get more done if she spent less time painting her nails.

He stared into the grinning face of Gonzalez. "Uh…"

She laughed. "Linn said you were a man of few words, but that is something else." She sat behind her desk. "Unless you've something else you'd like me to do, Linn has asked me to sort through these messages and see which ones require a response."

It didn't take the women long to be on a first name basis. "No, go ahead. I'm not your boss."

Her pretty smile never faded. "You are my superior in a way. I plan on making myself indispensable to this department." She bent her head over the pink slips of paper in her hand.

Steve scratched his eyebrow and took his seat. Had he

ever been that eager to prove himself? He couldn't believe so. Serious for as long as he remembered, Meaghan aka Queen Coral, had come the closest to getting him to loosen up. Look how well that went. He was starting to think he would remain a bachelor until the day a bullet took him down.

# Chapter 3

"I think you need to speak with your son, Martin." Devonne stared through the glass at his brother.

Martin scowled. "How'd you get in here?"

"Even prison guards have a price." Devonne tapped the glass with his knuckle. "Are you listening, bro? Because I'm serious. No blood of mine is going to the other side. He joins me or your family pays."

Martin leaned back. "You're bringing down the family."

"Kamal is mine."

"I raised him."

Devonne set his jaw so tight he thought his teeth would crack. "You might have been the big guy once, but now it's me." He thumped his chest. "You're in there, I'm out here."

Martin grinned, flashing his teeth against his ebony skin. "I won't be in here forever."

He'd never leave if Devonne had anything to do with it. He stood. "Have a good life, bro. I'm handling things out here."

Martin pounded on the plexiglass. "Hey. What are you going to do to my boy? Devonne!"

In answer, Devonne flipped his older brother the finger.

Martin's pounding and cussing increased, causing the guards to drag him away. Fitting. He might have been a great leader once, but he'd turned traitor, setting up one of his own in exchange for a light sentence. Nothing would ever make Devonne turn snitch. He'd die first.

~

Kamal stood on the corner waiting for the bus that brought Lincoln home. A dark, older model Cadillac cruised by. The window rolled down to reveal a grinning young hood.

An icy fist clutched Kamal's heart. He knew the guy as one of his uncle's. The gang member pointed a Glock in his direction.

Kamal squared his shoulders. Better him than Lincoln.

The hand holding the gun turned and fired five rounds into a boy around the age of thirteen who had just exited the drugstore. The boy danced like a puppet Kamal had seen once.

Screams filled the air.

Kamal threw himself to the ground and scrambled on his hands and knees toward the bleeding kid. Blood bubbled from his chest. Knowing the act was futile, Kamal pressed his hands over the wounds and watched as the caddy squealed tires as it sped away.

This was a warning. Because Kamal wouldn't do what his uncle said, an innocent kid died. He'd plead one more time to the cops. If they still refused, he'll go it all alone to bring his uncle down.

~

"Shots fired." Linn pounded on the conference room window where the others sat going over the day's duties. The 911 call had gone out over the scanner. Sometimes being late for work picking up bagels paid off. She hadn't gotten mired in daily activities yet. She dropped the bag on her desk and sprinted for her jeep.

Drew hopped in the passenger side while Steve and Gonzalez took the only squad car. Sirens wailing, they sped for the seedier side of town. Dread crawled down Linn's spine like liquid mercury. She prayed they wouldn't find Kamal lying bleeding on the sidewalk.

Drew reached over and took her free hand. He'd always been able to know her thoughts. "Don't get worked up over something that might not be."

She exhaled slow and deep before answering. "I know."

She stopped the jeep behind the squad car and rushed to where Kamal, covered in blood, slumped against the building. Lying next to him was the body of a younger boy.

Linn knelt next to him. "Where are you shot?"

"Nowhere." Kamal cleared his throat. "It's his blood. I tried to save him."

Linn put a hand on his head. "Stay put. We'll talk to you in a few. First, we need to take care of this young man, okay?"

He nodded, silent tears running down his cheeks. "I told you this would happen."

"Just wait." She got to her feet and hurried to help Steve prepare the crime scene. Every few minutes she glanced over to make sure Kamal had followed her orders not to move.

She hated leaving him next to the body, but the alcove he sat in was the safest place to be at the moment.

The bus pulled to a stop and Kamal's younger brother jumped off and darted to Kamal. Linn moved to intercept. "You can't go over there."

"That's my brother." He raised wide eyes to hers.

She squatted down to meet him eye-to-eye. "Do you know what a crime scene is?"

"Where something bad happened? Did something bad happen to Kamal?"

"No, and for that we are very grateful. There's a chocolate bar in the glove compartment of that jeep. If you can stay in the seat, you can have the candy."

With one more glance at his brother, the boy took off, closing the jeep door once he was inside. Kamal's gaze locked on the jeep like a lifeline.

Linn grabbed a water bottle from the trunk of the squad car. She ducked under the crime scene tape and set her aluminum case next to the body. "Drink this." She handed Kamal the bottle. "Want to talk while I do my job?"

"I'm going to join the gang. My uncle knows this is Lincoln's bus stop. This was a warning. Now, someone else's brother is dead. Mine is next." He twisted off the bottle top and drank half of it in one drink. "That's pretty much all I've got to say."

Linn used the opportunity of snapping photos of the scene to think through what she needed to say. "I think we need to talk about this first."

"What, ain't you got a CSI person?"

"No more money in the budget. We do what has to be done."

"That's what I'm talking about." He stood, holding his blood covered hands at his sides. "I gotta do what needs doin'."

She lowered her camera. "We'll talk more at the station. I promise. We'll get you cleaned up, something to wear, and—"

"No. I can't go there anymore. If I'm seen too many times—"

"We have to take you in to make a statement. I can make it look as if you went reluctantly." She reached for the handcuffs on her belt.

"Make it look good." Kamal turned to run.

Seriously? Linn set the camera down and took off after him. The boy was fast. She couldn't catch him. Drew took over the chase and soon brought the struggling young man to her.

"Really." She shook her head and cuffed him. "You were safe in the shadows." She opened the rear door of the squad car. "Watch your head."

"Been here before."

Linn slammed the door and resumed casing the crime scene. She hoped with everything in her that Kamal wasn't playing them.

~

Drew stared across the table at a clean, belligerent, dressed in his spare shirt, Kamal. "How do you know Devonne is behind the shooting? We've more than one gang close by."

"I recognized the shooter."

"How do you know you were the target?" Drew folded his hands on the tabletop.

"He pointed the gun at me first. I want to talk to the woman." Kamal glanced at the two-way mirror. "She listens to me."

"I'm listening."

"She's nicer."

"You got me there." Drew grinned and waved his hand at the mirror. "She's nice until you get her riled. Detective McFarland wasn't happy to have to chase you down."

Kamal shrugged. "Had to be real. My family's lives are at stake."

Linn entered the room and sat in the chair next to Drew. She mimicked his posture by folding her hands on the table. "You wanted to see me?"

"Don't play stupid. Are you going to use me or not?" Kamal's gaze hardened. "'cause I got other things to do with my time." He leaned closer. "Like keep my family safe."

"We're going to do everything in our power to help you," Linn said.

"Good. Then, I'm your new informant." Kamal crossed his arms.

Drew glanced at Linn's stern profile. He hated using a sixteen-year-old to gain information on one of the worst crime lords Arkansas had ever seen. It went against everything in him. But…the boy was going to join the gang to bring Devonne down with or without their help. It might as well be with.

"We'll be in contact as to where we can meet safely." Drew stood. "What you've agreed to do is dangerous. You could very well be increasing the danger to your family. But, since you're insistent, we'll do our best with what we have."

"I can go?"

"You can go." Drew motioned the boy forward. "Don't do anything more stupid than what you're already doing."

Drew followed him outside and glanced around, making sure no one sinister waited for the boy. He wanted to give him a ride home, but doing so would look too friendly. So, he watched like a mother hen until Kamal was out of sight.

"This isn't going to end well." Linn joined him on the steps. "I've got a bad feeling."

Drew learned long ago to trust her feelings. "We'll do our best. That's all we can do."

~

"I got your message." Kamal stood in front of his uncle.

"Which one?" Devonne stroked his chin.

Kamal's blood froze. "What do you mean?"

"I paid a visit to your father. He says hello."

Kamal clenched his fists. "Why are you involving him? He ain't here."

He shrugged. "I told you I would do whatever it took to get through to you. It looks as if it worked."

"That kid didn't have to die."

Devonne planted his hands palm down on the table and pushed to his feet. It suddenly occurred to Kamal how large his uncle actually was. Close to six-four and built like a linebacker, he leaned across the table, putting his face inches from Kamal's. "You should have joined me sooner, shouldn't you?"

Refusing to cower under the cold stare, Kamal squared his shoulders. "What's the big deal? You have plenty willing to do what you say. Why me?"

A slow grin, void of humor, spread across Devonne's face as he tossed Kamal an indigo-colored tee shirt.

"Because you're mine." He settled back into his seat. "Ask your mother. Now leave. I'll see you in the morning. Don't make me come looking for you."

# Chapter 4

Linn lay snuggled against Drew's side the next morning. Getting out of bed was the last thing she wanted when her main job from then on was to keep a young man safe while taking down a gang boss. "We need a vacation. Somewhere with just the two of us, sand, and the ocean."

"After this case. I promise. Maybe a honeymoon?" His eyes sparkled.

She twisted her lips. There would always be something. Not that she blamed him. She was as committed to her job as Drew was. Still, there were times she wanted to walk away from it and take a hiatus.

"As much as I hate to," Drew said, patting her hip, "we'd best get a move on. We need to find a way to use Kamal while still keeping him safe."

"That is going to be hard." She sighed and tossed off the sheet. "Is he coming in today?"

"He's supposed to. No guarantees with him, though." He bent over and kissed her before heading for the shower.

If Kamal didn't come to them, she would go to him under the pretense of checking on the younger boy. Blowing Kamal's cover would get him and his family killed. She couldn't live with that.

She made the coffee while Drew showered, then switched places with him, dressing in her uniform of dark pants and a blouse. She chuckled. The only thing that changed was the color of her blouse each day. Her mind flicked back to the first case she'd worked with Drew and how she'd pretended to go back to her old ways of exotic dancing in order to catch the killer obsessed with her. She much preferred her current wardrobe.

Drew nuzzled her neck as she swept her long hair into a ponytail. "How's the rookie working out?"

"She's okay." Linn closed her eyes, enjoying the feel of his lips on her skin. "Her constant chipperness drives Steve nuts, though."

"Most happy people annoy your partner." He gave her ear a nip, then stepped back. "Ready?"

"Steve isn't that dour." She playfully bumped him with her shoulder.

"Yes, he is." Drew flashed a grin and opened the front door. "His picture is next to the word in the dictionary. We need to find him a good woman to love."

"That hasn't worked out so well in the past." First, she chose Drew over her partner, then the next woman who showed promise turned out to be a psycho. Literally. Drew was right. Steve needed a woman to love.

She glanced over at Drew as they got in the car. He gave her a slow sexy smile that made her stomach flip. Five years ago, Linn would never have believed someone like him could love a woman with her sordid past, but here he was, professing his love daily and showing it in a million more ways with his actions. She doubted Steve could find a woman to come close to what she had, but she prayed he would. She wanted her friend to be as happy as she was.

"What's on your mind, gorgeous?" Drew folded his arms on the top of her jeep.

"I love you."

His smile widened. "Ditto." He motioned his head for her to get in, then did the same.

Steve met them in the parking lot. "Devonne recently visited his brother in prison."

Linn's eyes widened. "Is it possible the older brother is still the leader?"

"I don't think he ever was," Drew said. "Looks like we need to pay another member of the Williams family a visit."

"So, don't get comfortable is what you're saying." Linn crooked her mouth.

"Yep."

She turned to Steve. "Have Gonzalez dig up everything she can on the young man who was killed yesterday. Nothing is ever random with Devonne Williams." She yanked open the door to the jeep and climbed back inside. Nothing like taking off and running before she'd finished her first cup of coffee. Linn was not a happy girl.

An hour later, Linn and Drew stared through the plexi-glass window at Martin Williams. The man's gaze darted everywhere but at them. He was clearly frightened of something.

"If you're truthful with us, Mr. Williams," Linn said, "we can help you and your son."

"Devonne won't hurt Kamal, not if he can help it, but Lincoln is another story," he said quietly, leaning closer to the screen that allowed them to speak.

"I think you're going to have to give us a little more information. Why won't he harm Kamal?"

"Because Kamal is his son."

Linn hadn't expected that. "Why the ruse?"

Williams sighed. "Back when Kamal's mother was pregnant, my brother had angered the leader of a rival gang. Rather than have his child at risk, he asked me to claim him. Kamal is a good boy, I'm proud to call him son, but Devonne has gotten worse with me being locked up. He thinks he runs things now."

"Doesn't he?" Linn raised her eyebrows. Could Williams still be the leader from behind bars? It could happen, but she was under the assumption he'd changed his ways.

William's shoulders slumped. "I reckon he does, at that. You've got to watch out for my boy Lincoln. My brother will gun him down to teach Kamal a lesson."

"He already had one of his men shoot one boy," Drew said, crossing his arms. "Know anything about that?"

From the shocked look on the man's face, he didn't. He shook his head and closes his eyes. "Had to be a rival's kid."

"Not a lesson to Kamal?" Linn leaned forward.

"Sure, but Devonne always has more than one reason to do what he does."

Linn's phone buzzed. She glanced at the screen. "Does the name Perez mean anything?"

"The world has a lot of people by the name of Perez." Williams glanced over his shoulder. "I can't talk too much about that in here, not if I want to live to see tomorrow, but Perez is the one Devonne had a quarrel with sixteen years ago. There will definitely be retaliation if one of the man's kin was killed."

"But it was a rival of your brother's that killed the boy."

"It wasn't one of Devonne's or anyone working for Perez, unless…" Williams stood. "you're dealing with someone new."

Linn's blood ran cold. The danger to Kamal and his younger brother just expanded, and they had no idea who was responsible.

~

"Mom." Kamal shook his mother awake. "What does Uncle Devonne mean by me being his?"

"What?" She blinked and pulled the sheet over her face.

Kamal yanked it down. "Wake up and answer my question."

She groaned and pushed to a sitting position. "Oh, my head."

"I'll get you some aspirin. What did he mean?"

His mother finally met his gaze. "I guess you're old enough to know the truth. Devonne is your birth father. Martin said you were his for your own safety against someone named Perez. That man went clean years ago."

Everything Kamal had known was a lie. "Lincoln?"

"He's Martin's." She put a trembling hand on his arm. "Martin is your dad in every way that matters."

Tears stung Kamal's eyes. No wonder Devonne insisted so strongly that he join the gang. He probably wanted *his* son to take over the operation someday. Well, *this* son had other plans for his life, and they didn't include a life of crime or years behind bars.

He went to the kitchen, returning with aspirin and a glass of water. "Here. Maybe you should stay in tonight."

"I've got to make money, son. I have no other skills."

"I'll ask Devonne to help us. If you and him were together once before—"

She shook her head. "I won't be his woman again."

"You'd rather spend time with a lot of men?" He crossed his arms, ashamed for what she'd become. "I'm making money, Mom. With welfare, food—"

"It ain't enough." She made a shooing motion with her hand. "Leave me alone. I'm tired."

Heart at his knees, Kamal checked on Lincoln, who watched cartoons on the television, then opened the front door to head to work. He hated leaving them, especially knowing how vulnerable his younger brother was. His mother had made her fate, but for a child to be in danger because of the sins of the father and mother was almost too much for him to bear. Maybe he could take his next paycheck, do a few jobs for his uncle, then take his brother and disappear. He stepped onto the porch and came face-to-face with the chief-of-police.

Kamal did the only thing he knew to do under the pretense of joining the gang and that was run. He jumped off the porch and sprinted down the cracked sidewalk, the chief on his heels. He darted through one of the few stores still renting DVDs and Blu Rays, knocking over a display, and charged through the back door. When he felt safe enough they wouldn't be seen, he stopped.

"Son, this pretense of yours is going to kill me," Chief Wayne said, bending over to catch his breath. "You sure can run."

Kamal grinned. "Gotta make it look good."

"We visited your father today."

"You mean my uncle." He swallowed past the lump in his throat. "I found out today."

Chief Wayne put a hand on his shoulder. "I'm sorry. I came by to let you know that Detective McFarland will be coming by your place in an hour to take your family into protective custody."

Kamal listened while the man told him about a possible third-party threat. "I can't go. Devonne would hunt me down."

"No, you can't, but your mother and little brother can. We'll keep an eye on you the best we can, but we'll have to take them. Tell Devonne your mother was arrested, and your brother placed in foster care. That should keep them safe for a while."

It could work. "Alright. I'll skip work today and be home, pretending to hide from the authorities when they show up. Then, I'll head over to Devonne's." The thought left a sour taste in his mouth.

He arrived home a few minutes before the authorities and knelt in front of Lincoln. "Some people are coming to take you away. You have to go with them."

"Why?" He turned away from his cartoon.

"Because I won't be able to watch out for you for a while."

"Mom can."

"No, she can't." He sighed as the doorbell rang. "Listen, to me. I'm not here. You don't know where I am. I'll come see you when I can." Devonne ducked into a closet and pulled the door closed, leaving just enough room to peer out.

Lincoln sent a puzzled glance his way, then went to answer the door. "Hi."

"Hello." Detective McFarland handed him a candy bar. "I didn't forget. Where's your mother?"

"Sleeping." He grinned and unwrapped his treat, something Kamal couldn't provide as often as his brother would like.

"You'll need to go get her." The woman smiled. "I'll wait here."

When Lincoln ran to the bedroom, a man in shirt and tie joined the detective. "I hate these kind of calls."

"Me, too."

Kamal's mother shuffled from the bedroom in rumbled cotton pants and tee-shirt. Her eyes widened at the sight of law enforcement and she started to race away. The man grabbed her arm, pulling it behind her.

"I'm sorry, ma'am, but you're under arrest for prostitution."

"What? Kamal!"

"It doesn't appear as if your older son is here," McFarland said. "We'll keep an eye out for him. Come with me, Lincoln." She held out her hand.

Lincoln glanced again at the closet before slipping his small hand into hers. "Okay."

Kamal blinked back tears, hoping, praying, he'd see his family again. The next step he needed to take would be a dangerous one.

~

It broke Linn's heart at how easily the little boy

followed her. A child should be more concerned for its mother, fight to stay with her. Lincoln came along like an obedient puppy while his mother fought and cursed on the way to Steve's car. She hadn't missed his repeated glances toward a closet, either, knowing Kamal was there, keeping a watchful eye on things.

She prayed for the young man's safety and wisdom for her, Drew, and Steve to make the right choices in bringing Devonne to justice without any more loss of life.

She buckled Lincoln into the backseat, trying not to shudder at the chocolate on his hands. Seats would wash. "Ready? We have a very nice home for you to go to." Linn knew just the right woman to keep an eye on the little guy.

A former neighbor of hers, Mrs. Richards loved children. She wasn't a foster parent, thus not in the system, and wouldn't be easily located up on the mountain. As a former schoolteacher, she could keep Lincoln up on his schooling. The boy couldn't be safer.

"See you back at the station," Linn told Steve. Not even her partner knew where Lincoln was going, only her and Drew. She hated keeping any information from Steve, but the boy's safety was more important than her partner's feelings. She'd explain it all when danger no longer loomed.

Half an hour later, she stopped in front of red-brick house. Mrs. Richards, short, plump, and smiling, stepped onto the porch. "Is this my guest?"

Linn took hold of the boy's hand and led him to her. "This is Lincoln. Thank you for letting him stay with you. I'm sure the two of you will have a lot of fun together."

"I'm sure we will." Mrs. Richards held out her hand. "I just made a batch of cookies, and I think there are some clothes around here that will fit you. Do you like Spiderman? I have some action figures waiting for you to play with."

"Really?" Lincoln's face brightened. "I've never had one."

Linn's smile faded. When this was all over, she'd make sure that little boy had all the silly little things that made children happy. "I'll come see you in a few days."

"With Kamal?" His eyes shined bright in his dark face.

"If I can." She bent and gave him a hug, again sad that he hadn't asked after his mother. "Thank you," she told the older woman.

"I'll keep him well cared for. Now, go and do whatever it is you need to do."

Linn nodded. She fully intended to make sure some people paid for the death of a young man.

# Chapter Five

After a restless night, tossing and turning, Linn left Drew sleeping and entered the precinct early. Steve and the rookie, Lydia Gonzales already poured over what little they knew in the conference room. "Good morning." Linn hung her jacket over the back of a chair.

Lydia glanced up and smiled. "There's fresh coffee on."

"Bless you." Linn made a beeline to the coffeepot on a sideboard. "Are y'all getting anywhere?"

"Nope." Steve shook his head. "Until Kamal gets back to us with some information, we're at a standstill. Do you want us to go talk to Williams?"

Linn finished preparing her coffee with cream and sugar, then faced him. "I doubt it would do any good, unless…" She blew into the hot drink. "You act as if you're looking for Kamal. Say he's wanted in questioning regarding that young man's death and he's disappeared."

"Should I mention the mother and brother?"

"We'll play that part by ear." She leaned against the end

of the table and studied the case board. They now knew with certainty that the dead boy was a Perez, but not the leader Perez's child. Most likely a distant relation. No criminal record, good school attendance, passable grades, nothing to warrant the boy being targeted. It appeared as if Kamal was right, and the other boy had been sacrificed as a message to him.

"Lydia, you stay and see what you can dig up on Devonne and Martin Williams. Try to decipher the dynamics between the two. Steve and I will go see Devonne."

"Like old times." Steve grinned. "Pounding the pavement together."

She laughed. "Walking into dangerous situations, you mean. The man won't be happy to be woke up this early, but maybe we'll catch him off guard." She transferred her coffee to a travel mug before donning her jacket. "I'm driving."

"Of course. You always do." Steve followed her to her new jeep and slid into the passenger seat, clicking his seatbelt into place. "The only time I get to drive is when I'm not with you."

"You should be used to it by now." She grinned, backing from her designated parking spot.

Devonne Williams might hold "court" in a rundown business complex in a neighboring city, but he lived on well-groomed acreage surrounded by a white rail fence and an iron gate. A sprawling ranch house sat back on the land, shaded by oak and magnolia trees. Crime paid very well, apparently. Not for long. Linn would do whatever she could to run the gangs out of her city.

Steve whistled. "This isn't a penthouse in New York."

"Not a mansion in California, either, but it could be."

The gate opened as they approached. "I wonder why there's no guard or the gate doesn't require a code."

"Maybe he's expecting someone." Steve studied the area around them. "Kamal, maybe?"

"That's a good assumption." She drove up the winding drive and parked in front of the house.

Devonne Williams stepped onto the front porch wearing a tribal patterned silk robe, a mug in one hand, a cigarette in the other, and a smile on his dark handsome face. A gold-plated tooth winked from the corner of his mouth. "Looks like I've got company," he said as Linn and Steve approached.

"We'd like to ask you a few questions, if you've got some time," Linn said, pasting a smile on her face.

"For you pretty lady, I've all the time in the world. Have a seat." He waved a hand toward a couple of Adirondack chairs.

"We're looking for your nephew, Kamal." Linn declined the offer of a seat and stood at the top of the stairs. She didn't trust the man not to make a move and needed to be able to retaliate. Plus, with her standing and him sitting, she felt as if she had the upper hand.

Steve stood at her side. "A young man was killed at Kamal's bus stop yesterday. When we arrived, your nephew was covered in the other boy's blood. Would you know anything about that?"

Devonne took a drag off his cigarette and blew a leisurely puff into the air. "All I know is that the two of you raided my sister-in-law's house yesterday, arresting her and carting the youngest boy off somewhere."

"We didn't see Kamal," Linn said. "Have you?"

"You've asked that question twice now." He chuckled. "Getting desperate? No, I haven't seen the boy in a day or two. I'm sure he'll turn up once he finds out his little brother is gone. He dotes on that boy."

Linn handed him a business card. "Please let us know if he does, Mr. Williams."

"I might, and I might not. My nephew is soft, Detective. He didn't kill that boy."

"Do you know who did?"

"Nope." He stood, towering over her by at least six inches. "But someone is stomping on my turf, and I intend to find out who."

"I'm sure the Perez's want to know as well." Refusing to be intimidated, she met his glare, her own smile not wavering. "Thank you for your time." She slowly turned and headed back to the jeep, Steve keeping pace with her.

Once inside the car, he asked, "Do you believe him?"

"I do." She kept her gaze on the big man watching them. "He doesn't know where Kamal is at the moment, but he is expecting him. He seemed too angry about someone invading his territory to be the one responsible for shooting that boy."

"He's going to be a problem with us getting to the bottom of all this."

"Yep." She turned the key in the ignition and drove back to the station.

~

As soon as the Detective's jeep turned the corner out of sight, Kamal stepped from the bushes and marched to face his uncle.

"About time, boy. I've been wasting time talking to

those pigs." Devonne turned and entered the house, expecting Kamal to follow.

His heart in his throat and a prayer he could carry out the ruse without detection, Kamal did as expected. Inside the house filled with black leather furniture and expensive decorations, he stood at attention and waited.

"The pigs were here asking whether you killed a boy at the bus stop."

"I didn't kill him. A car pulled up, fired several rounds, and sped away."

"Did you see who pulled the trigger?"

Kamal shook his head. "It happened too fast."

"Think boy!" Devonne smacked him upside the head. "White, brown, black…?"

"Black, I think." He glared and restrained from rubbing his head. "The windows were tinted. All I saw was a hand and the gun."

Devonne paced the floor. "I need more information. I want you out on the street asking questions. If we have a new rival, I need to know. Don't let me down. You hungry?"

Kamal nodded. "We never have enough food in the house."

Devonne muttered something unflattering about his mother, then yelled for someone named Rosie to fix breakfast. "You've time for a shower. There ought to be clothes to fit you in the closet. Use the back bedroom."

"Okay." He shuffled his way to the room and tossed his dirty clothes in a hamper. While the water in the shower grew hot, he studied his new room. Bars on the windows showed he'd not be sneaking out. He'd come and go through the front door where he could be watched. Devonne might be his birth father, but he didn't trust his son to do what he was told.

After showering and dressing in clothes that would have kept food on his families table for a week, he sat down to a large breakfast of eggs, bacon, and toast. It took all his will power not to wolf the food down like an animal. All the while, Devonne watched with narrowed eyes.

"You haven't said a word to me about the pigs taking Lincoln."

Kamal's hand froze halfway to his mouth, the eggs falling back onto the plate. "I ain't been home. Why'd they take him?"

"They arrested Felicia. Probably put the boy in the foster care system. Where you been hiding?"

"Nowhere in particular. Just wandering the streets."

Devonne laughed. "Not a lot of streets to wander in Upton Falls."

"But there is a lot of woods. I know how to be invisible."

"Chicago taught you something."

Yeah, like what kind of man his father was. "I reckon." He finished eating, then stood. "I'll be back by supper."

"Hold up, son." Devonne tossed him a set of car keys. "Take the caddy. You'll cover more ground. Everyone knows the car so they won't strip it when you park it somewhere."

For the first time in a long time, Kamal smiled. He'd always loved the black Cadillac. "Thanks!" He could go just about anywhere now on the pretense of snooping for Devonne. Of course, he'd have to throw the man a nugget now and then, but he had a rare freedom with a car. It wasn't until he got behind the wheel that he realized driving a very recognizable car could be dangerous. If Devonne had undiscovered enemies, they could think he drove instead of Kamal and attempt to assassinate.

Was that what Devonne planned for Kamal? Did he want his son out of the picture?

He gripped the steering wheel and glanced toward the house. Devonne smiled and waved from the front porch. Closing his eyes and taking a deep breath, Kamal turned the key in the ignition, releasing his breath when the car's engine turned over without incidence.

He drove to the interstate and the state's capitol. With no firm destination in mind, he cruised the city's most violent neighborhood in search of one of Devonne's people. They might not know anything, but they could at least attest to the fact that Kamal was asking questions.

Parking behind a dumpster in the alley of a smoke shop, Kamal locked the car and pocketed the key. Going further on foot would be safer. The least people saw the Caddy the better. He ducked into a shop and bought a cheap throw away phone, then stepped outside and surveyed his surroundings.

Three gang members laughed, smoked, and shoved each other on the street corner, quieting as they eyed Kamal approaching. He gave them the chin tilt "What's up" and joined them.

"You're on the wrong side of town," one of them said. "What's a lily-white black boy like you doing in these parts?"

"Devonne sent me to find out who killed that Perez kid." Kamal hardened his features.

"You joined up?"

Kamal gave a sharp nod. "I'm tired of working for pennies." He gave a cold smile. "Found out Devonne is really my father, not that loser Martin. As his son, I can't very well stay out of the family business, can I?"

The news visibly shocked them. "I want you…boys…to keep your eyes and ears open. There's a new threat to us, and Devonne wants to flush them out."

"We don't know nothing." The young man said.

"You'd best be learning, then." Kamal squared his shoulders and continued on, ducking into a corner gas station. The old man there knew everyone in the neighborhood. "Hey, Mo."

"Kamal? Ain't seen you around here for a good long while."

"I'm digging for news on the killing of the Perez boy." Kamal leaned against the counter. "Know anything?"

Mo exhaled sharply. "You'd best stay out of things, young man. This is no life for you."

"It is now." If he wanted to live to see his seventeenth birthday anyway.

"Yeah, I know something. A couple of guys from the Bahamas moved in a couple of streets over. Said they're wanting to claim this as their territory. Word is they plan on doing so by pitting the Williams' against the Perez's. My guess is the Perez boy was killed as the first wave of attack." He reached over the counter and gripped Kamal by the neck of his tee shirt. "You might be next, fool. Leave this place. Start a new life somewhere else."

One day, after this was all over.

# Chapter Six

"Word on the street is some hoods from Jamaica moved in."

Linn sighed. "I don't like this Kamal. It's too dangerous."

"I'm in up to my gonads now. Too late to turn back. Gotta go. Devonne's coming." Click.

Linn stared at the cell phone in her hand, then over at Drew. "New gang in town, just as we figured, and they want to take over."

"Who are they?" He peered over the rim of his coffee mug.

"Bahamas, Kamal said." She pushed away from his desk. "Steve and I will pay another visit to Devonne. See what he knows."

"I've already sent Steve and Lydia to the neighborhood Devonne's thugs run. I'll go with you." He grabbed his jacket from the back of the chair.

Lucy, their receptionist rushed to his office. "Shooting

in the park."

"Change of plans," he said, darting out the door.

Drew drove, lights flashing to the park next to the river. Steve and Lydia were already on the scene, keeping spectators back. "We're going to be stretched too thin with this case."

"When does Lydia's new partner arrive?"

"By the weekend." He shoved his door open. "He's an experienced cop getting close to retirement. He'll be good for us."

Linn nodded and followed him to where a young Hispanic man lay near the water, his body riddled with bullet holes. She squatted next to him and opened her case. After slipping on a pair of gloves, she took his fingerprints, then straightened and started taking photographs. She moved around the body, snapping pictures from every angle, before turning to the surrounding area. Another young man sat in the ambulance, a stark white bandage around his arm.

With a motion to Drew as to her next move, she stepped up to the young man. "Hello, I'm Detective McFarland. Are you up to answering a few questions?"

"Is Juan dead?" The boy swallowed hard. He couldn't be more than sixteen. A child fighting a war.

"I'm afraid so. Did you see who did this?"

"The East End."

Devonne's people. "You're sure?"

"They were black."

"Did you see their colors?"

He shook his head. "Just an arm and gun out the window."

Same MO as the bus stop. "Listen to me. There's a third

party involved here who is trying to pit the West Side against the East. Tell your boss not to retaliate against the East. It wasn't them."

He jerked his gaze to hers. "I ain't seen no one else."

"You'll have to take my word for it. What's your name?"

"Miguel Rodriquez."

"What were you and Juan doing here?"

His face darkened. "Smoking a little weed, skipping rocks, nothing bad. Then, this black Caddy, like Devonne drives, pulls up and opens fire on us. I ducked behind those rocks, but Juan wasn't fast enough. How am I supposed to tell his mother he's dead?"

"That isn't your responsibility. We'll take care of that. You focus on yourself and consider getting out of this walk of life before you end up like your friend." She handed him a business card and asked that he call her if he finds out anything that would help in their investigation, then returned to where Drew and the others questioned other witnesses.

"His story matches Kamal's," she said. She glanced to where news reporters waited, one more anxious than the others. "I guess I'll go give Alan Barker a statement before he makes something up."

"Lydia and I are headed to the East side," Steve said. "We'll catch up at the precinct later."

She nodded and marched to where the reporters waited on the other side of yellow tape.

"A gang shooting?" Barker thrust a microphone in her face.

She scowled and slapped it away. "You know better than to force that thing on me. It's a gang shooting, but not between the East and West."

"A third one?" His eyes widened. "Who?"

"Undetermined. That's all we know at this point."

"So, we have a phantom gang pitting the other two against each other?"

Sometimes she forgot how quickly he put the pieces together. "Allegedly." She turned and rejoined Drew. "Now what?"

"We go question Devonne again."

~

"What do you have for me?" Devonne clapped Kamal on the shoulder.

"Bahama people on our turf." He tried not to cringe from the man's touch.

Devonne slowly removed his hand and lowered to his overly large leather chair. "My past has caught up with me." He leaned his head against the chair back.

"What does that mean?" Dread rippled through Kamal.

"It's none of your concern."

"It is." He clenched his fists. "This is affecting the whole family."

"Fine." Devonne poured himself a glass of whiskey from the crystal decanter on the end table beside his chair. He downed it in one gulp, then poured another. "Your grandfather was just starting out in this business, prostitution mostly. Martin and I were his main men, although we weren't much older than you are now. Anyway, one of the girls who worked for us was beat up by someone."

"You."

He shrugged. "She turned snitch. Anyway, I roughed her up too much and she lost the baby she was carrying. My old man sent me away for a while hoping it would all die down.”

“Why rear up now?”

“Some homie who fancied himself in love with her said he’d get even one day. I wonder what took him so long?”

Kamal’s guess was the man spent time in jail and just got released. He froze as the doorbell rang.

“Get out of sight,” Devonne ordered. “It’s the pigs again.”

Kamal ducked into the bathroom off the main room, leaving the door open enough to peer out as Devonne opened the front door, and the chief and detective entered.

“Good morning, Mr. Williams,” Detective McFarland said. “This is our Chief of Police, Andrew Wayne. We have a few more questions, if you don’t mind.”

“I still haven’t seen Kamal.” He resumed his seat. “Sit.”

“We’ll stand,” the chief said. “One of the Perez gang was shot dead in the river park this morning.”

“I don’t know anything about that.”

Another shooting? Kamal sagged against the wall.

“Is there someone in there?” The detective asked.

“With the door open?” Devonne laughed. “I wouldn’t think so. We’re a little more civilized than that.”

“Word is that a new group has come to our fair city,” the chief said.

“Really? What does that have to do with me?”

“They’re pretending to be some of yours, right down to the black Cadillac you drive.”

That silenced Devonne for a minute. “That means Perez will be gunning for me. I demand protection for me and my family.”

"Perhaps you could go into hiding as it seems Kamal has," the detective suggested.

"I ain't gonna run scared."

~

Steve liked the fact Lydia had no problem letting him drive. What a change from Linn. "What made you want to be a police officer?"

She cut him a sideways glance, her hazel eyes sending his heart in a direction he definitely didn't want to go. Not with his past bad luck with women. "My grandfather was a cop, my father was a cop…it made sense for me to follow in their footsteps since my brother decided to be a teacher. I like to see justice done. Why did you?"

"Same reason."

"I've followed your career." She smiled. "The Photographer case, your twin brother and all, very creepy. Then, Queen Coral, well, the last year or so has been very exciting for you and Linn."

"Hmm." Exciting? More like terrifying. "This sleepy little town has definitely woken up the last few years."

"Now, I get to be a part of it all."

He liked her enthusiasm and hoped it didn't dim when things got rough. He parked his SUV in front of a gas station on the East side. "We go on foot from here. This is one of the only places my car won't get stripped. The people here respect the owner. He's also a good source of information about what goes on around here."

"Are we visiting him first?"

Steve nodded and shoved open his door. He led the way into the station and waited for it to clear out before approaching the counter.

"If you're looking for Kamal Williams," the man said, "he was here yesterday. I told him to get out of here. If he took my advice, he's long gone."

Steve glanced at Lydia, then back at the station owner. "What did he want?"

"He was asking questions about who was responsible for killing the Perez kid. I told him there was a new gang in town from the Bahamas."

"Sir, it would be in your best interest to stop talking about these people. The East and West don't bother you, but there's no telling what these new people will do," Steve warned.

The man pulled a shotgun from under the counter. "I'm ready."

Lydia put her hand over the weapon on her hip.

"It's okay," Steve told her. "Sir, put that away. Officer Gonzales is new to our town and might take offense to having a gun pointed at her."

"Right. Big city people and their aversion to guns." He put the weapon back under the counter. "I'll keep my eyes and ears open for more news. All I know at this point is they're mimicking the East Side. Keep an eye out for a black Cadillac."

"He didn't tell us anything we didn't already know," Lydia said.

"No, but he confirmed what the victim told us this morning." Steve stood in the center of the station's lot and glanced up and down the street. The more questions asked, the more visible they were, the more likely the new gang would make a showing. The killing wouldn't stop until East and West met in a bloody battle, then the newbies would come in and take over when the other two gangs were weakened.

"Do you think Linn knows where Kamal is?" Lydia stepped up beside him.

"I'm sure of it. She squirreled his mother and brother away, and most likely made some plan with the boy." It irked that she hadn't included him in those plans. Once, they'd shared everything together, but that was before Wayne. Before Steve's brother's obsession with Linn almost killed her.

As he and Lydia rounded the corner, a black Cadillac slowed. The window rolled down to reveal the barrel of an automatic rifle.

"Get down!" Steve tackled Lydia to the ground as bullets sprayed around them.

Pain ripped through his thigh, another stab through his arm. Lydia squirmed under him, finally throwing him off her. She aimed her Glock and fired until the chamber fell empty. The car sped away, a dark blue tee-shirt dropping out the window.

She glared at Steve. "Don't ever treat me as something fragile again. If you hadn't thrown me to the ground, we could have both fired on them."

Great. Another strong-willed woman. "I'm hit."

"Oh." Her eyes widened, and she crawled over to him, pulling a radio from her belt. "Officer down, Corner Gas, East Main."

# Chapter Seven

"They got away." Lydia glared to where paramedics were putting Steve into an ambulance. "Because Chavez thought he had to play hero and cover my body with his."

"Sounds familiar." Linn frowned, then turned to Drew. "What's that?"

"A dark blue or purple tee-shirt?" He held it out to her.

"They threw that out the window," Lydia said.

"I think that color might be considered indigo." Linn opened an evidence bag. "Their colors?"

"Gives me something to dig into." Lydia limped for Steve's car, tossing over her shoulder. "Tell Chavez I'll be by the hospital later. Oh, and the arm aiming out the window was Caucasian."

What in the world happened to her town? "You ought to get checked out," Linn called. "You've got some nasty road rash."

The rookie waved a dismissive hand and climbed into the driver's seat. The tires squealed as she pealed from the parking lot.

"She's as strong-willed as you are in regard to not being treated differently than a man." Drew grinned.

"Same as me, she has a job to do. Gender can't be a factor." Lydia had filled them in on everything that transpired, from speaking with the station owner to the gun shots. Things were escalating faster than the authorities could prepare. From children to cops, no one in Upton Falls was safe. They needed to bring down this new gang, and fast.

"I'll take care of this, if you want to go be with Steve." Drew tossed her the keys to her jeep. "I'll find a ride back."

"I can drop you off first." She caught the keys in her right hand. "What I want to know," said, climbing into the jeep, "is why target Steve and Gonzales?"

Drew fastened his seatbelt. "This might be a stretch, because Perez is a common name, but our rookie's mother's maiden name is Perez."

"How did I not know this?" Linn shot him a startled look.

"Did you read her file?"

"Not yet."

"It isn't a secret."

Linn steered toward the Interstate. "I doubt she has gang affiliations. That could have prevented her from being a police officer. Who do the Bahamians have a beef with? Williams or Perez? The more Perez's are targeted, I'm starting to wonder if we've been chasing the wrong dog."

"That's what they want us to think. They're starting a war, and we're going to be stuck in the middle."

"We don't have the manpower for that." The hair on her arms stood up.

"They know that." Drew put his hand over hers. "We'll manage, same as always. I'll see if I can't get the FBI to send in a few agents."

As a former agent, Drew had pull where Linn didn't. His buddies would come, if they could. Her primary focus would be on keeping the residents of her town safe. And Drew. She's almost lost him before, it wouldn't happen again.

Linn dropped Drew off at the office, then headed to the hospital to check on her partner. With the flash of her badge, a nurse led her to a curtained alcove where Steve waited to have stitches.

"Nothing serious. They gave me a local, so it doesn't even hurt." He moved the bed to a sitting position. "Doc said to use a crutch until the stitches stop pulling. There's nothing to keep me from working."

"I didn't think you'd stop even if you had surgery." She grinned and sat in the chair next to the bed. "Officer Rodriguez said the shooter was white."

"I didn't see him. Why shoot at police officers casing a scene?"

"Drew thinks it might be related to Officer Rodriquez. Her mother's maiden name is Perez."

"That's a long stretch."

She shrugged. "Who knows anymore? It's worth checking into. Have you read her file?"

"Bits." He sighed and rested his head against the pillow. "I'll read it thoroughly once I'm out of here."

Linn glanced up as Lydia entered the room. "I'll take off. You're in good hands." She smiled at the officer, patted Steve's shoulder, then left the room wanting very much to talk to Kamal about how recruiting young men worked.

She sent him a text to his burner phone, then joined Drew back at the station.

~

"Don't do that again." Lydia sat in the seat vacated by Linn.

"Do what? Get shot?" Steve tilted his head. "I'll do my best."

"Treat me like a woman." Her eyes flashed.

"But you are a woman." Call him confused. Maybe she identified as male?

"I know that, but first and foremost, I'm a police officer. If you hadn't played hero, you might not have gotten shot."

"Or, one of us might be dead." What was with her and Linn? Couldn't a beautiful woman be treated as one even if she was law enforcement?

A nurse came to him, sparing him the need to say something that would anger Lydia. "Let's get you stitched up." She went to move the blanket covering him.

"Oh." Lydia jumped to her feet, a blush staining her cheeks. "I'll, uh, wait for you outside."

The nurse laughed. "I'm only exposing your leg."

Steve preferred the pretty officer waiting outside. He didn't want her to see him in such a vulnerable state. Why was that? He'd sworn off women.

Once she'd finished stitching him up, the nurse flung open the curtain for Lydia to reenter. "I'll be right back with your release papers and care instructions."

Steve barely had his pants zipped before Lydia joined him. Standing on one leg had taken a toll. The numb leg wouldn't support his weight which meant there'd be no walking out of the hospital. He'd need help.

He glanced at Lydia, her smooth brow now creased. For one of the rare times he did, he wished it were Drew there to help. Even the chief was better to put his arm around than Lydia.

Not a problem. No more women, remember? Which meant he would look at the rookie as nothing more than a badge. Right.

The nurse returned with a wheelchair and release papers. She shook her head at Lydia's offer to push the chair. "I'll see you out. You can take it from there."

Outside, Steve got to his feet, making sure not to pressure on his numb leg. Lydia shoved her shoulder under arm and helped him the few feet to her car. He caught a whiff of a floral-scented cologne and took a deep breath. The scent came from her hair.

A slight breeze blew a strand free of her ponytail and across his face. It slid across his skin like silk. His heart skipped a beat as Lydia glanced up, smiled, and stepped clear. "Front seat or back?"

"What?" He blinked a few times to clear his head.

"Where will you be more comfortable?"

"Front if the seat is all the way back." She wasn't his chauffeur.

She nodded and moved the seat. "Steady." She reached for him.

"I got it." Ushering the door, Steve managed to half fall into the front passenger seat. The gearshift jammed him in the ribs and took his breath away.

"You okay?" Lydia shot him a concerned look. "In pain?"

"I'm fine." He ground the words through his teeth and straightened.

"Can you feel your leg?"

"Not yet." He put his hand over the stitches.

"Then home it is." She turned the key in the ignition.

"What?"

"The chief said that if you couldn't walk that I was to take you straight home and tell you not to attempt to come to work until tomorrow." She grinned, her eyes twinkling, clearly enjoying being able to tell him what to do.

No matter. He'd spend the time going through her file. He flashed her a grin, then settled into his seat.

She studied him for a moment, a suspicious glint in her eyes before shrugging and pulling onto the road.

~

Kamal's burner phone vibrated in his pocket. He itched to check it, but had no reason to leave the room. The other gang members would ask too many questions unless it was to go to the bathroom or kitchen, and he'd already eaten and gone to the bathroom.

He tossed a tennis ball in the air, catching it with ease. The only people who could call that phone was the detectives or the chief.

"Why are we sitting around?" He got to his feet and faced the other six boys.

"We get paid to be ready at any minute," Jay said. "What if Devonne needs us and we're not here?" He shook his head. "That ain't good. We stay until we hear otherwise."

Kamal had given up his job at the grocery store to sit around bored. He couldn't get any information on his uncle that way.

Devonne entered the room and frowned his way. "What's up with the hyperness? Relax between jobs. That's what keeps you alive."

He sat again. "It's boring."

"Play chess." His uncle grinned. "I do have something I want you to do. I've heard there's a Jamaican gang, wears indigo, trying to pit us against the Perez's. Find out if that's true. Whatever beef we have the East, and the West shouldn't be shooting each other if there's a different threat." He snapped his fingers. "I need it yesterday, boys. Go."

Kamal didn't need to be told again. He dashed from the room and to the older model Taurus given to him to drive. He peeled away from the curb before any of the others could hitch a ride.

At a stoplight, he glanced at the phone. Yep, the detective had said she needed to meet with him. He replied the where. Fifteen minutes later, he parked behind a church and waited.

Detective McFarland pulled alongside him and rolled down her window. "Any news?"

"No. Done nothin' but sit around all day." He rested his wrist over the steering wheel. "Now, I'm supposed to be trying to find out about the new gang."

"Which is why we're here." She took a deep breath. "We're ninety-nine percent sure there's a new gang. They fired at a couple of our law enforcement and tossed out their colors. Indigo, dark purple, there's some dispute on the color." She laughed. "The shooter was white."

Kamal widened his eyes. "Not unusual, but not common. These country boys tend to steer away."

"That's my question. What would entice someone to

join a gang?"

"You mean other than poverty or lack of family?" He frowned. "Money would do it. I'm making a lot more than I was at the grocery store."

"You think the gang could be recruiting drug addicts?"

He nodded. "Easy convert. Disposable." Most would do anything for a fix.

The detective thought for a minute as if trying to decide how much to tell him. She bit the inside of her cheek. "It was a tee shirt thrown out. Detective Chavez caught a bullet. Two Perez boys dead in the park. You found this out by an informant you met in the alley. You didn't catch the man's name, but he's white and homeless. Got it? That explains to Devonne who told you." She smiled. "A good man doesn't give up his informant. Tell him that if he presses the issue. He'll understand the respect aspect."

"Thank you." Kamal cleared the clog from his throat. No one had cared enough to cover for him before.

"Anytime, buddy. We're partners." She flashed a grin and pulled away.

Kamal sighed, wishing he didn't have to put up an act in order to keep his family safe. He glanced at the detective's lights in the rearview mirror. Someday, he'd be law enforcement and help put scum like his uncle away.

Right now, he was nothing more than a sixteen-year-old who didn't know whether or when he'd be discovered and killed.

# Chapter Eight

Steve sat in his leather recliner and put the footrest up before opening the rookie's file. He ridiculously hoped he wouldn't find anything to raise any red flags. Drew wouldn't have hired her if there were any, would he? Although as short staffed as the department was, he might have been inclined to overlook some things.

He took a sip of the coffee he'd sat on the end table and scanned the pages. He froze upon seeing Lydia's grandfather's name on her mother's side. Perez. Emilio Perez to be exact. Former gang member turned informant before someone knocked him off.

Could the new officer be connected to this gang war? Steve didn't believe in coincidence. He picked up the phone and called the office.

"Chief Wayne."

"It's Steve."

"How are you feeling?"

"Fine. I'll be in tomorrow. I'm wondering whether you

think there's any link between Lydia's grandfather and what's happening now?" He set the file on his lap.

Drew chuckled. "Just now reading her file? Maybe, but her grandfather has been dead for twenty years. Seems like a long stretch to me. Perez is a common name. Someone would really have to go digging to find out that information."

True. Maybe no one would be that interested. With the new gang pitting the other two against each other, maybe everyone was too busy to care about the new officer. "Hopefully. Thanks." Steve hung up and drummed his fingers on the arm of the chair.

The chief wasn't a stupid man. He'd have considered the same things Steve thought about. Still, he couldn't shake the feeling that something wasn't quite right with the new hire. He needed to get close to her, befriend her, see if she'd come clean about her family history.

The drumming of his fingers increased. Would she accept a dinner date with him? He wasn't adverse to pretending to be romantically interested, but getting involved with someone he worked with, even on a pretense would be frowned upon.

Officers of the law were supposed to trust and respect each other. He pressed his lips together, then grinned. He knew of a restaurant where a lot of the local crime figures ate. Good food, and he could invite Lydia under the pretense of staking out the other diners.

He snatched his phone from the table next to his coffee cup and gave her a call. "Want to go out to dinner tomorrow night?"

"Uh." Silence screamed. "Is that wise since we work so closely with each other?"

At least she didn't say no. "Oh, sorry. It's a local hangout for the crime rings, but the food is good or so I've heard."

"Okay, then." Relief laced her words. "Undercover type of thing. Yes. That sounds good." Her voice perked up. "I've never gone undercover."

"Not exactly undercover as we won't be pretending to be anyone but who we are." He chuckled. "Tomorrow night. Seven o'clock. Meet me in the parking lot of the office." He hung up and rubbed his hands together. Step one of clearing, or somewhat convicting, Lydia. Not that he thought her guilty of anything, but if this did pertain to her grandfather in any way, then the chief needed to relieve her of her duties until it was all behind them.

~

After checking emails and returning messages, Linn grabbed her jacket and gun, slinging both over her shoulder on the way to her jeep. Just because Steve was down, didn't mean the work stopped. She needed to find out more about the Jamaicans, find out exactly what they wanted with her town.

She left a text on Drew's phone and drove to the other side of town. On one corner mingled young men in royal blue, another green, no sign of indigo. From the body language of those she could see, they were all on high alert. Shifty eyes, hunched shoulders, hands patting pockets as if to reassure themselves they still carried a weapon. Things could get real ugly real quick.

She pulled to the curb in front of a vacant used video game store and got out of the car.

Kamal, wearing a royal blue baseball cap, drove slowly

past. His eyes widened when he spotted Linn. He parked a few spaces ahead of her and joined the other boys in blue.

Linn strolled across the street acting as if she weren't in a hurry. The skin on the back of her neck prickled from the stares of those in green on the other side of the street.

"Gentlemen." She smiled, glancing from one to the other, not lingering on Kamal. "Mind if I ask you a few questions?"

They all stepped back except Kamal, showing her without question who was in charge. "What kind?" Kamal crossed his arms. "We don't like talking to pigs."

"Well, since I don't oink and I don't have a curly tail, then we should get along just fine." Her grin widened. "I'm not here for any of you. I want to know about the indigo gang."

"Join the club."

"You're out here every day. You must know something. Where they hole up? Who's in charge? Why Upton Falls?"

"They're like ghosts. You're out here doing the same thing we are. Trying to find out information. You can ask the Greenbacks, but I doubt they know any more than the Royals do." His posture relaxed slightly. "What we do know is that they want all of us dead."

"Why?"

He shrugged. "That's for law enforcement to find out, ain't it?"

She drew air sharply through her nose and nodded. "You boys be careful. People are dying." She turned and marched across the street to question the Greenbacks.

Their leader met her at the curb. "That's far enough."

She arched a brow. "Just here to help and ask what you

know about those wearing purple/dark blue."

"Nothing 'ecept they want to rid the streets of all of us."

"How do they recruit?"

His eyes widened. "No idea. I don't plan on turning."

"The royals are mostly black. The Greenbacks are mostly Hispanic, although both do have a few from other ethnic groups, but there's word on the street that the Jamaican's might have a few white boys."

He nodded. "Look. You want to know about that, go check the homeless living at the abandoned campground out by the lake. Lots of druggies there who'll do almost anything for a few bucks. I bet that's where they're getting their recruits."

"Thank you. You've been very helpful." She headed back to her car, halting, hand on the gun in her holster, as a black Cadillac moved at a snail's pace past her. She narrowed her eyes to see inside but the dark tint on the windows made it impossible.

Feeling like a sitting duck, she quickly got back in her car. Every eye on the street followed the black vehicle as it moved past. Every spine straightened. Hands went for pockets.

Linn held her breath, expecting a gunfight, and releasing her breath in a huff when one didn't arrive. Instead, she pulled from her spot and got behind the Cadillac not caring if they knew she followed. Sooner or later, they'd stop, and someone would come talk to her. She hoped it would be a conversation rather than a bullet.

After about a mile, the car in front of her stopped. Linn set her gun on the dashboard in front of her.

The passenger side door opened, and a young man in

indigo approached the passenger side of Linn's car, motioning for her to roll down her window.

She obliged. "I'm Detective—"

"We know who you are. The Indigos know all the law enforcement in this town." He flashed a smile, revealing a gold tooth. "What do you want?"

"To know why you're in my town."

"To make it ours." He frowned. "You been nosing around too much."

"You're trying to start a gang war."

He laughed. "Saves us some time."

"Who's your leader?"

"Ajani Brown."

Linn stiffened. She'd heard of the crime lord. Things had just escalated to a dangerous level.

"I see you know of him. Go on, Detective. You don't want to mess with us." He slapped the car before marching back to his.

Linn swallowed against a suddenly dry throat and turned the car around. Thirty minutes later, she stood in front of Drew's desk.

~

"Ajani Brown."

Drew glanced up from the report he studied. "He's here?"

"Yes." She nodded. "Leader of the Indigos."

He sat back in his chair. "You know this how?"

"I went asking questions."

"Alone." He gritted his teeth. Why was she so stubborn?

"My partner was unable to come with me, you were out of the office, and there's a job to be done." She hitched her chin.

"Linn." He growled and folded his hands on top of the desk so tight his knuckles ached. "What is wrong with you?"

Her gaze darkened.

"Why are you so persistent in doing things alone? I hope that now you know who we're dealing with, this won't happen again." She could've been killed. The Indigos rarely left a body behind. Most people simply disappeared.

"At least now we know who we're dealing with. The Royals and the Greenbacks are running scared. I think they'll work with us."

"I don't want them to work with us. I want them all gone." He took a deep breath to steady his emotions. Sometimes, keeping work and private life separate seemed impossible, especially with them living together, being engaged, and planning to get married. None of which would happen if she got herself killed.

He sighed. "What else?"

"One of the Greenbacks confirmed that the Indigos are most likely hiring druggies from the homeless park out by the lake."

"Okay, we'll check it out in the morning, early." He speared her with a glance. "Do not, and I repeat, do not go there without me or Steve. Preferably with me as Steve will be using a crutch for a few days. There's no argument here, Aislinn."

Something flickered in her eyes at him using her full name. "Yes, sir, chief." She spun and marched from his office.

He didn't enjoy putting her in her place, but she needed to stop going off on her own. Yes, she was a brilliant detective. The department was lucky to have her. He was lucky to have her. But, if she kept going off alone, no one would have her. Somehow, he needed to make her realize that fact.

She'd been a detective long enough now not to act as she did before going through the academy. She hadn't been a rash rookie in a very long time.

He put his head in his hands and sighed again, knowing he'd have the cold shoulder when he got home. Once she cooled down, he'd be able to explain to her why he'd reprimanded her. He shut down his computer and followed her home.

The sound of banging pans lured him to the kitchen. He paused in the doorway and prepared for the backlash now that they were out of the office.

"Don't look so worried." She smiled over her shoulder. "I understand. I really do. You worry about me as much as I worry about you, and that, my darling is a lot. A whole lot." She set down the pan in her hand and moved close enough he could wrap his arms around her which he did.

Her gaze searched his face. "I can't promise not to go off alone. In fact, I probably will, but all I can say is that I will weigh the consequences first."

His hold tightened. "That isn't good enough. I can't survive if something happens to you."

"Then we're even." Her smile trembled. "I lost you once, Drew, remember?"

Of course, he did. A person doesn't forget being slammed against a van by an explosion and being brought back to life. "I don't want to go through what you did. I'm too selfish." He leaned his forehead against hers. "Brown is one of the worst, Linn."

"I know," she said softly. "I'll be very careful. I promise."

He wanted to believe her, and while he knew she meant her words, she wouldn't be able to keep the promise.

# Chapter Nine

Linn and Drew marched shoulder to shoulder toward the boxes and tents that housed at least fifty people. The homeless had chosen concrete slabs as if they were nothing more than campers renting a space for the weekend.

The sour odor of marijuana permeated the air. Linn doubted that was the only illegal substance being used. She wrinkled her nose and approached the first tent that was more duct tape than canvas.

A pile of clothes moved. A head of tangled gray hair popped out. Watery blue eyes stared up at them. "What?"

"I'm Detective MacFarland. This is Chief Wayne." Linn flashed her badge. "We're wondering whether you've seen any strangers around? Newcomers? Young men you haven't seen before?"

She shrank back into the pile of clothes. "I stay to myself. Ain't seen nothin'."

Linn glanced at Drew. "Use your magic," she mouthed. She hadn't met a woman yet that he couldn't charm.

He chuckled and hunkered down next to the woman mindless of the dirt on his slacks. "Ma'am. What's your name?"

Blinking like an owl, she faced him. "Alice. Ain't nobody called me that in a very long time."

"Well, Alice." He smiled. "Boys are dying. Being shot down in the streets by some bad people. Men who we suspect are recruiting boys from this very camp. Now, a woman as sharp-eyed as you is bound to have seen something." He pulled a twenty-dollar bill from his pocket.

Her eyes lit up.

"Could you see it in yourself to help us? We're kind of at a loss, and we could really use someone like you."

The woman looked like a puppy about to be offered a treat. "You mean help the police?"

"Yes, Alice. I can't think of anyone better to take on the task."

"Let me think." She tapped her head with the palm of her hand as Linn shot Drew an amused glance.

"Okay. Yes. It started out with two men wearing dark shirts. I think they were blue? Anyway, they came at night. There aren't any lights out here, so I can't be certain. Dark-skinned, spoke with an accent. Braided hair, I think." The hand against the head moved faster.

Linn reached out to stop her only to have Drew take the woman's hand in his. "You're doing great, Alice."

"They passed right on by me. Barely spared me a glance. They only spoke with the younger men. A few of them went with them that night. They ain't been back. Them or the men."

"Do you know the names of the boys that left with

them?"

"Carl, Danny, and Willy. That's it." She snatched the money and scuttled into her tent.

Drew got to his feet. "I doubt we'll get any more information from Alice or anyone else, but we can try."

Linn glanced at the now suspiciously void of people spaces. "I think you're right." She exhaled heavily and started down the road to the next site.

"Hello?" She peered into an empty refrigerator box turned on its side. Empty. So were all the others. While her and Drew had talked with Alice, the others had melted into the shadows. "This isn't typical behavior even for homeless people. These folks are scared."

"They'd better be with Brown sending his men around." Drew studied the tree line, then turned his attention to the lake as smooth and placid as a mirror. "We won't find out anything more here."

"What about the high school? Maybe these boys aren't homeless, but come to do drugs out of the sight of their families and peers."

A twig snapped behind her. Linn whirled, hand on her gun. A rabbit hopped from behind a trashcan and toward a brick building almost covered with foliage.

"Let's check the restroom." She headed that way, Drew falling into step beside her. Several of the tents were close enough for the occupants to have taken refuge in the building.

"Let me go first." Drew put an arm in front of her.

She rolled her eyes, but stepped back. Let him play the hero once in a while. With her heart in her throat, she stayed as close behind him as she could without stepping on his heels.

Drew pushed open the door.

Someone slammed it from the other side.

He fell back, taking Linn down with him.

She landed hard, the breath leaving her in a whoosh.

Springing to his feet, Drew gave her a quick glance. "Okay?"

She nodded and waved him on while she lay there gasping like a banked fish.

Withdrawing his weapon, Drew shoved the door open with force this time. "Police! Come out of there. Do not make me come in after you."

Three men shuffled from the restroom. All were dirty and so skinny, Linn couldn't see how they'd managed to knock a man as big as Drew off his feet. By now, she stood, providing backup, and glared at them. She'd be surprised if she hadn't suffered a cracked rib.

"Why hide?" Drew waved them to stand against the building.

"Trouble," one of them muttered. "Right here in River City."

Wasn't that a musical? "What kind of trouble?" Linn asked.

"With a capital T." He spit the word T. His comrades remained mute. "Foreigners."

Linn didn't expect to get much from him. "Care to elaborate?"

"Ghosts come in the night."

Drew returned his weapon to its holster. "We're done here. His rambling has confirmed the camp has had visitors. We won't get anything more."

"Steve and I will visit the high school tomorrow," she said as they headed back to his car. "Unless you want to send him along with Lydia."

"Since the main thing on my schedule is stopping these gangs from killing each other, I'm free to go with you." He glanced at her over the top of the car. "Steve and Lydia can question the Royals and Greenbacks regarding these three missing boys."

"They aren't missing if no one has filed a report." She slid in the passenger side.

"Which sounds very strange, doesn't it?"

~

Steve straightened his tie, then rang the doorbell of Lydia's apartment. Running late, she'd asked him to come pick her up rather than meet somewhere. He had to keep reminding himself they weren't on a date. Only work. Then why did his heart flip when she answered the door in a scarlet red dress with lips to match?

"You look great. Where do you hide your gun?" Stupid.

She lifted the side of her dress to reveal a gun holster. "It's a bit uncomfortable, but it works."

The sight of her shapely leg almost stopped his heart altogether. "Ready?"

"Absolutely." She brushed past him, leaving a whiff of a musky cologne in her wake. "I'd say you look nice, too, but you're always in a suit." She laughed.

His face warmed at the semi-compliment, and he rushed forward to open her car door. "Thanks."

"Do you ever lighten up?" She asked.

"My partner would tell you no." Did he? Not really. When was the last time he went fishing, read a good book?

When he got off work each day, he continued working on the latest case or watching all the news channels.

"Is your partner correct?"

"Pretty much." He'd tried relaxing once until Queen Coral got her clutches on him. Relaxation had almost killed him.

He drove to the Italian restaurant where he'd heard Devonne frequented, along with his rival, Juan. They had their own tables on opposite sides of the building and did their best to pretend the other wasn't eating in the same room. At least that's the rumor he'd heard.

Parked, he held Lydia's door open again and offered his hand to help her out. Placing his hand on the small of her back, they strolled into the restaurant and were escorted to a table for two near a window that overlooked a garden and a fountain.

"Nice place for crime lords," Lydia said, taking her seat.

"Supposed to have good food." He smiled and opened his menu.

After they'd ordered, a glass of wine in front of each of them, he glanced around the room, not spotting either Devonne or Juan. "Doesn't look as if either of our persons of interest are eating tonight."

"The night is still young." She smiled. "Mind if I ask you a question?"

"Only if I can ask one in return." He raised his glass to his lips.

"How did it feel to find out you had a twin that killed women who looked like your partner?"

Not expecting that question, he almost choked. Keeping his face as impassive as possible, he took his time setting his glass down. "About as one would expect. A bit of a shock." He met her gaze. "How did it feel growing up in the shadow of a crime lord?" He arched a brow.

She laughed. "You've read my file. My grandfather got out of that business when my father was born. He didn't want to raise his son that way."

"Is it possible that this war against the Perez's could be linked to you?"

"Ah, there's the real question." Her smile faded. "I've considered that idea and can't see how. We've not had any trouble at all since my grandfather quit that business."

"No one simply leaves that lifestyle, Lydia."

"Well, my grandfather did." She crossed her arms and glanced out the window, then straightened. "I think we've a deal going down."

He followed her gaze to see a young man in a blue tee-shirt speaking with someone in a green shirt. The two looked friendly enough at first, then green shoved blue and took off at a run.

"Let's go." Lydia bolted to her feet and out the back door.

Steve groaned and gave chase. Why couldn't he find a woman that didn't seem to relish danger at every turn? A gentle soul he could come home to at night, cuddle with, and discuss his day?

"Halt! Police." Lydia had kicked off her heels.

The woman was fast, Steve would give her that. "Officer Rodriquez, cease."

She cast a look over his shoulder that told him she thought he was kidding. "Seriously?"

"Absolutely." He stopped.

She returned to his side. "They're getting away."

"There is nowhere for them to go except over a ten-foot fence. This is private property owned by the restaurant owner. One way in, one way out. The boys have to come back this way. There's no sense in you charging blindly into danger." He narrowed his eyes. "Now, if you'd like to follow me…"

He led her down the path at a more leisurely pace. He stopped as something rustled behind a thick bush. "Come on out. There's no way to escape."

Blue came from one side of the path, Green from the other. They glared at Steve and Lydia, then each other.

"Mind telling me what's going on?" Steve showed his badge.

"Nothing," Blue said.

"Yeah." Green nodded.

"Looked like you wanted to fight and thought better of it."

"So?" Blue's brow furrowed. "Look. We used to be friends, now we're on opposite sides. All I wanted was to know if his sister was okay. We dated once. He told me to mind my own business, and I got mad. That's it."

Steve bit back a grin. "Isn't it dangerous for the two of you to be seen together? If we saw you through the window, then you can bet someone else did."

Their eyes widened.

"Dude." Green shook his head. "We messed up bad. Did you see any of the brothers inside?"

"No, but that doesn't mean they weren't there. That little push, then the race through the garden isn't fooling anyone. Go home. Stay there for a while."

Both boys' lives would be forfeit if anyone suspected their loyalties lie anywhere but with their gang.

# Chapter Ten

Linn peered over her steering wheel the next morning. "Is that Kamal? I didn't think his uncle would allow him to keep attending school."

"Let's see if he'll talk to us." Drew opened his door. "If he's here, he'll know the three missing boys."

"Hopefully." They marched toward the cluster of teens.

Kamal frowned and crossed his arms. "Haven't you harassed us enough?" He glanced around the group receiving head nods in response.

"We're looking for three missing boys. Carl, Danny, and Willy. We don't have their last names. Heard of them?" Linn asked.

"Of course. This school isn't that big, and it's my job to know everyone." Kamal hitched his chin, wariness shadowing his eyes. "I don't know anything about them missing. Besides, it might be best if you talk to Mr. Horn, the principal."

Reading the plea in his eyes, Linn nodded. She wouldn't

jeopardize his cover any further. She handed him a business card. "Give me a call if you remember anything."

As she moved away, she heard one of the boys ask, "Why is she always asking you questions?"

Linn cast a glance at Drew. They'd have to be a lot more careful.

Inside, they were ushered immediately into Mr. Horn's office. The tall, thin man closed the door behind them. "You're looking for missing boys?"

"Yes, sir." Drew folded himself into a chair.

"I heard they joined a new gang." The principal folded his hands on his desktop. "Those three are always in some trouble or another. Have they been reported missing?"

"No, and that's the strange part." Linn leaned slightly forward, locking gazes with the man. "I'm assuming the boys haven't been at school?"

"You'd assume right."

"Have you contacted the parents? It has to have been a while."

"We've left messages on their phones." He pulled three folders from a stack on his desk. "Here is their contact information. No fathers to speak of, busy mothers. Maybe you'll have better luck. Did they not join the gang?"

"That's what we're trying to find out." Linn nodded and got to her feet, scooping up the folders. "Let us know if you hear anything." Irritation pricked like biting ants. Why didn't the principal seem more concerned?

She glanced around the now empty lawn of the school before getting back into her jeep. "Feel like hunting down some mothers?"

"Yep." Drew clicked his seatbelt into place. "We

suspect the boys joined the Indigos, but we don't know for certain. It bothers me that no one has reported them missing. If the school is leaving messages on the home phones, wouldn't a parent wonder where their child spent their days?"

"You would think." She turned the key in the ignition. "Where to first?"

He set the closest address into the GPS. "Willy's. The other two live in the same complex nearby."

She took a deep breath and headed in the right direction. These sort of calls, the ones where she felt as if she called out someone on being a bad parent, was not a favorite aspect of her job.

Willy lived in a trailer park. Linn drove at a snail's pace over a rutted road badly in need of repair, past homes in sad need of paint. Grass grew over children's bikes. A lone red ball sat under a rusty swing set.

She exhaled heavily and parked in front of what might have once been a trailer painted a cheery sunflower yellow. No cars were out front. All the blinds were closed, although a few were missing strips. Her heart ached at the feeling of giving up the place exuded. Here goes nothing. She exited the car and marched toward the trailer.

Drew peered in one of the windows with missing blind slats. "It's dark. Doesn't look as if anyone is home."

Linn knocked on the door. No answer. She turned the knob. The door opened with a slight squeak. "Hello? This is Detective MacFarland. Anyone home?"

"She's at work."

Linn turned to see an elderly woman in a faded housedress walking a poodle in need of a haircut. "When does she get home?"

The woman shrugged. "Should've already been home. Works at Lou's. Most times, she brings some worthless man home with her. Maybe she went to his place this time. Either way, if you don't see a dented-up Ford Taurus then she ain't home."

"We're actually looking for Willy."

"Ain't seen him in days. Figure he run off."

"Why would you think that?" Drew tilted his head.

"Iffen he is here, all they do is yell at each other. What boy wants a no-good mama?" She strolled away with her dog.

"Guess we're headed to Lou's," Drew said.

"I reckon we are." Her phone rang. She glanced at the screen, saw it was Steve, and put it on speaker. "What's up?"

"Last night, Officer Rodriquez and I went to dinner at that Italian place outside of town and saw two—"

"Hold on." She grinned. "Did you say you two went to dinner?"

"Yes, on a stakeout. Focus, Linn."

She shared an amused glance with Drew. "Sorry. Proceed."

"There were two boys in the garden, one Royal, one Greenback, cousins, fighting over a girl. I'll text you what information I found on them. I think someone needs to keep an eye on them. Lydia and I might not have been the only ones to notice."

"Just because they were seen talking doesn't mean they're in danger."

"Sure, it does. Gotta go. We're on the east side asking questions. Word on the street is something big is about to go down." He hung up.

Something big could be bad or very bad. Linn drove to Lou's. "You take the lead here." The bikers that frequented the place wouldn't like a woman questioning them, detective or not.

~

The school day dragged. At lunch, Kamal ditched and drove to his uncle's. His buddy was right. The detective asked him too many questions with others around. He'd have to let her know to keep any contact to the burner phone. Kamal wasn't that good of an actor. Sooner or later, he'd slip up and then all he'd worked for would be for nothing.

"Why aren't you in school?" Devonne glanced over from the kitchen table. "An education is important."

"You don't have one." He grabbed a soda from the fridge.

"I didn't have time. You do." His uncle's eyes narrowed. "You found your brother and no-account mama yet?"

"No. Don't care to." He popped the top and chugged the drink, so tired of the acting. He really needed to find something that would put Devonne behind bars, end the gang wars, and get his family back. "Besides, I ain't going to college, so what's the point?"

"The point is that I said so."

"You're not my..." He'd forgotten that Devonne was his biological father.

Devonne slammed to his feet. "I don't want those words to ever leave your mouth again or you'll regret them. Now, get your lazy rear back to school. I don't want to see you until four o'clock. Then, I've got a job for you."

Shoulders slumped, Kamal drove back to school. He hopped the fence and entered through a back door left unlocked by the kindergarten rooms. He hid in the bathroom until the bell rang, then entered the next class with his classmates.

His attention couldn't focus on the English paper in front of him. All his mind could dwell on was what kind of a job Devonne had for him.

~

Drew led the way into a bar filled with cigarette smoke. A bartender leaned against the bar talking to a woman in a tight skirt and low-plunging blouse. Another woman wiped tables. Two leather-wearing men sat at a table and played checkers.

He headed for the bar. "Looking for a Winnie Jones."

"That's me." The woman propped a hand on her hip and flashed a smile until he showed his badge.

"Mind if we ask you a few questions?"

She glanced at the bartender, who nodded. "I'm off work anyway. Follow me." She led them to a table on the opposite side of the room. "What's this about?" She sat and crossed her arms.

A long night of work had left mascara rings under her eyes. A fleck of lipstick stained her front teeth. Her dark roots showed through bleached blond hair. She smelled of cheap perfume and sweat.

"Any idea where your son is?" Drew asked as he and Linn sat across from her.

"Ain't seen him all week. Figured he's been staying with a friend."

"Haven't you been receiving the messages from school

saying he hasn't shown up?"

Her eyes widened. "My phone ain't working right. Are you telling me no one knows where my boy is?"

"We suspect he's joined a new gang in town." Linn slid a business card across the table. "You son and his friends have been hanging out at the homeless campground and doing drugs. They were seen leaving with two men associated with the gang. No one has spotted them since."

"Willy is always in trouble. I know he's like the marijuana, but a gang…" she shook her head. "I never would've believed it."

"Does Willy have a cell phone?" Drew studied her face, getting the impression the woman really didn't have a clue where her son could be.

"I can barely afford my own." She glanced from him to Linn. "What do we do?"

There were a lot of things he wanted to tell her, but none of them nice. "Please do your best to get a hold of your son, then call us." He tapped the business card. "This is very important, Ms. Jones. Your son's life could be in danger. We'll also pay a visit to the families of his friends." Although, he was pretty sure, he'd get the same type of answer.

"I have no idea how to find him. Wait a minute." She got to her feet. "Roy!" She waved over one of the bikers.

"Yeah." He shuffled toward them.

She explained the situation. "Can your guys find my boy?"

He studied her face, then turned to Drew. "The Jamaican's?"

"Yes, sir."

"Ain't they dangerous?"

"Very."

"Willy could be in danger?"

"Without a doubt."

The man nodded. "We'll see what we can do."

Linn handed him a business card. "Don't engage with any member of the gang. Simply call us when you find him."

"Alright." He pocketed the card and waved to his buddy. "Y'all remember this next time you want to harass us about being where we aren't supposed to be. You'll owe us."

Drew laughed. "You find this boy and his friends, Carl and Danny, and we'll negotiate."

Back outside, Linn faced him. "Think they can find them?"

"Those guys are all over this town. If the boys are still here, they'll find signs of them." It was a big if. Chances were the boys were the ones doing the drive-bys, but there was as big of a chance that they had been killed as an initiation for other boys.

Things were going to get very bad before they got better.

Linn cruised by the high school on the way back to the office.

Kamal, hands shoved in his pockets, crossed the parking lot. He glanced up and kept walking. Defeat marred his face.

The boys posture reinforced the idea that they never should have used him to bring down his uncle.

# Chapter Eleven

Steve ignored the frowning looks Lydia cast his way, keeping his attention focused on the road and the call they headed toward. Someone had reported shots fired at the park near Main.

"Are you giving me the cold shoulder because I took off after those kids last night?" If looks could cut glass, he'd be bleeding all over the upholstery.

"I'm not giving you the cold shoulder." He sent her a quick glance. "I'm thinking of the job ahead."

She made a noise in her throat. "I don't know how Detective MacFarland puts up with you. I'm a police officer. Forget that I'm a woman and let me do my job."

As if he could. That fact was much harder now that he'd seen her in that red dress. Her uniform didn't do much to hide her femininity either. He sighed. "I'll work on treating you as a good ole' boy."

Her laughter pealed through the car. "Those words sound funny coming from you. What brought you to this

Southern town anyway?"

"Work. Then, I got partnered up with Linn and stayed."

"Because you love her."

He shot her a shocked look. "I thought I did."

"Well, my heart broken hero, look at that crowd." She directed his attention to a lot of people filling the parking lot. "They've most likely contaminated the scene…if there is one. Could be some of those good ole boys having fun."

Maybe, but Steve didn't think so. Three gangs warring for turf would be anything but good. He pulled between the park and the crowd, receiving several angry gestures from the bystanders, and got out of the car. "Who called?"

A woman with a small dog in her arms stepped forward. "I did. I live right over there." She pointed to a small brick house. "I heard the shots and called, then came to see whether anyone needed help." Her chin quivered. "Buddy here found a body under a juniper bush behind the swing set."

Steve closed his eyes for a second, then opened them and nodded at Lydia. "Let's check it out, then get some tape up to keep people away."

She squared her shoulders and followed him across a playground circled with houses and apartment buildings that had seen better days.

Steve widened his eyes at the sight of Drew and Linn marching toward them. "Thought you two had other things to do."

"One of which happened to be at that apartment complex. I've got a gut feeling," Drew said, "that one of the reasons we're here is under that bush."

Steve hoped not. He hunkered next to the bush. He

didn't have to part the branches to see the pale face of a young man. With another heavy sigh, he dug in the pockets for identification and pulled out a driver's permit. "Carl Fredericks." The boy had been shot several times in the chest.

"This looks an awful lot like an initiation," Lydia said softly. "Bring in outsiders and find out who has what it takes to join the family." She made quote marks with her family. "Do the deed and you're in."

"That's quite a stretch, isn't it?" Steve glanced at Drew.

"Linn and I were starting to believe the same thing. There's been no sign of Willy Jones. We haven't visited the home of Danny Sawyer yet. Do the two of you want to do that task and Linn and I will finish up here?"

"Sure." If they didn't find the other two boys soon, they'd wind up like Carl if they weren't already. He jerked his head for Lydia to follow.

A few minutes later, they knocked on the door of the last known address of a boy named Danny. After a few minutes of knocking, a woman in a large, faded tee-shirt answered the door. She blinked at them a few times before her eyes widened at the sight of Lydia's uniform.

"Yeah?"

"Ms. Sawyer?" Steve showed his badge.

"That's me."

"Mind if we come in and ask you a few questions?"

"Is this regarding the shooting in the park? I don't know anything about that." She moved to close the door.

"No, ma'am, it's about your son, Danny."

She clutched the neckline of her shirt. "Is that him lying dead out there?"

"May we please come in." Doors opened up and down the stairwell as heads poked out, curious to know their business with this woman. "We can talk with more privacy."

She stepped back to allow them entry, then closed the door. "Have a seat and tell me where my boy is. He obviously isn't staying with friends."

Steve exchanged a look with Lydia before facing the woman again. "Danny hasn't been at school in quite a while, ma'am. Were you aware?"

"Yeah, but the boy is sixteen. If he don't want to go to school, who am I to make him? I quit in the ninth grade."

Steve scratched his forehead rather than say what he really wanted to say. And that was that as the boy's mother, it was her job to make sure he attended school and graduated. At least try to do the best of her ability.

"We don't know where your son is, Ms. Sawyer. We were hoping you would know. He left the homeless campground with two men over a week ago. No one has seen him since."

"Then, he's gone. My boy is dead." Tears welled in her eyes. "He would come home by now for money if nothing else if he were alive."

"We don't know that for a fact." Lydia looked around the room. "Is there anyone in the complex he hung around with?"

"That Carl boy. He hung out with a boy named Willy, but he lives in the trailer park." She plopped onto a sofa that not even throw blankets could hide the rips. "My boy isn't…wasn't real social. I don't know what tense to use."

"Hold onto hope as long as you can." Lydia smiled. "Give us a call if you hear from him."

The woman nodded, focused on her hands dangling between her knees. "Yeah, you call me when you find my boy dead."

~

Linn tied crime scene tape around the base of a tree, then stretched it to a basketball hoop and around until she'd circled the area. It didn't take a genius to see the four bullet casings from a 9-millimeter littering the ground. Despite what Drew said, she didn't totally buy the idea these boys were used as an initiation.

Maybe this boy's death was simply the fact that he refused to do something as ordered. She really wanted to continue to believe the world wasn't as bad as it seemed right now.

Once the tape was secure, she wandered the playground in search of clues. There were far too many footprints in the sand. Too many to determine which belonged to a shooter. Thankfully, most of the children who lived near were in school. Things could have been a whole lot worse.

"No one saw anything." A muscle ticked in Drew's jaw. "In broad daylight."

"Someone just isn't talking." With two apartment complexes three stories high and at least twenty homes circling the playground, someone saw who shot this boy. "Fear would make them bite their tongue. This is worse than The Photographer or Queen Coral."

"Yes, because kids are dying." He squared his shoulders. "We need to let Carl's mother know before she hears it from someone else. Word travels fast in this town."

"I hate that part of the job." Thankfully, it hadn't happened in over six months. "I'll go while you wait for the

ME. It doesn't take two of us."

"You sure?" His gaze searched her face.

She nodded. "By the time this is finished, she'll have heard."

"Okay. I'll catch a ride back to the office."

"I'll swing by here when I'm done in case you're still here." With heavy steps, she made her way back to her jeep rather than walk to the apartment.

She climbed to the third floor and knocked on the address for Carl. A woman young enough to have had the boy in her teens answered the door. "Ms. Fredericks?"

"Yeah." She shoved inky black hair away from her face. "I'm late for work."

"This will only take a minute." Linn doubted the woman would go to work after hearing the news. Without waiting for an invitation, she stepped into the woman's apartment. Clean, sparsely furnished, but what she had was in good condition. "Please sit, ma'am."

Worry flickered in her eyes. "Carl?"

"When was the last time you spoke to him?"

"Before dawn. He called me, sounding frightened. Said he was coming home."

Linn jerked, surprised at the news. "This morning?"

"Yes. He didn't come." She lowered herself slowly to the sofa. "Said he'd gotten mixed up in some trouble, which isn't new to him, and wanted to come home. He was crying." Silent tears rolled down her cheeks, marring her makeup.

Linn sat next to her. "Carl's body was found this morning in the park."

"The gunshots?"

"Yes."

She hiccuped. "He almost made it home."

The statement shattered Linn's heart into a million pieces. She swallowed against a tight throat. "I'm so sorry. We'll need you to come to the morgue this evening to identify his body."

"But, you said it was him." Hope shined in her eyes.

"He had his driver's permit in his pocket."

"Okay." Defeat laced her words. "I'll be there. Please see yourself out." She got to her feet and shambled down the hall.

~

Kamal's hand trembled as he pulled the gun from his pocket. Devonne had ordered him to hold up the corner convenience store. A test. One he didn't want. One he could fail. "Empty the register into a bag. Hurry." He glanced at the camera, wanting the authorities to see his face.

"Don't shoot me." The middle-aged man opened the register. "You know I can't open the safe, right? Don't shoot me because I can't open the safe."

"Hurry up!" Antonio, the one ordered to go with Kamal, waved his gun in the man's face. "You press an alarm and I'll shoot you in the face."

The man grabbed fistfuls of cash from the register and stuffed them into a paper sack with the store's logo printed on the side. "You came before I locked this up. Ten minutes later, and I'd have nothing in here."

Which was the plan. His uncle knew almost everything that went on around his turf. "Come on, dude." If he kept dawdling, Antonio would shoot him. Kamal didn't want to be involved with murder.

Antonio grabbed the bag, then turned his weapon on

Kamal. "Shoot him. Devonne said so. If you don't, he'll have both of us killed, and he'll track down Lincoln."

Kamal stared into the wide eyes of the man. "I'm sorry." He aimed at the man's leg, shut his eyes, and squeezed the trigger, wincing at the sound of the shot.

"Let's go." Antonio grabbed his arm as sirens wailed in the distance. "Shake it off. It's part of the job. The man means nothing."

He meant something to someone. Kamal sprinted for his car and squealed tires away from the store. Anger burned through his veins. Devonne had known what it would take to get him to pull the trigger.

For the sake of his little brother, Kamal needed to end this.

# Chapter Twelve

Linn sat at her desk, twirling a pencil. Drew had left before she woke that morning with no word as to where he planned on going. The pencil flew through her fingers, barely missing Steve's head.

"Find something to do." He frowned and shook his head, returning his attention to his laptop.

"Did Drew tell you what his plans were today?"

"No." Steve straightened. "Is that why you're fidgety? I'm sure it's important. No need to worry."

"This isn't like him." Don't worry? Ha. She did nothing but since that explosion that almost took him from her.

Lydia glanced up from her desk. Without commenting, she ducked her head back down, no doubt hoping Linn would expand on the conversation.

Well, she wouldn't. She wasn't comfortable airing too many personal tidbits about herself to the new rookie. Not until she knew the woman could be trusted.

She sighed and sent an email to Mrs. Richards to check

on Lincoln. She didn't have to wait long before she got a reply.

He's good. A real sweetheart, but he does miss his brother. One thing worries me, though. There's an old rattletrap of a truck that drives by here twice a day like they're going to work and coming home. The thing is, Linn, is that no one lives or works up the road from me. Thought you should know.

Hmmm. Could be something, could be nothing, but with the lives of two boys at stake, nothing could be left uninvestigated. She replied back to only let Lincoln out back of the house to play where no one from the road could spot him, and to text her the description of the truck, before she glanced at Steve. "Want to pay a visit to Mrs. Richards?"

He glanced at Lydia. "Will you be alright here alone?"

She rolled her eyes. "I'm not going to answer that question."

Hiding a grin, Linn left the room and let Lucy know to contact her when the chief returned.

"Why are we heading up the mountain?" Steve slid into the passenger side.

"She said there's been a strange truck driving up and down her road. I want to see if I can catch a glimpse of it. I told her to text me the description. A dark green older model Ford 150 with a bashed in right rear light." The woman was a marvel. "There's a big scratch down the left side."

"She needs to be on the force."

"This is the reason she's the perfect guardian for anyone. Nothing escapes her attention." She steered the car west and up the mountain.

"There really shouldn't be anyone around her place

uninvited. Especially this time of the year." She slowed their speed for the multiple switchbacks as they headed up. "Her property butts up against government land that no one uses except during deer season. She's the only house, and there are no businesses."

"I can see why you want to check it out." He turned slightly sideways to face her. "You and Drew having problems?"

"Not really…yes. He's been bent out of shape since I went to the east side alone."

"I don't blame him. This time, I'm on his side. You are very reckless."

"I do my job!" Her neck heated. Why were men so insistent sometimes on treating a woman as something fragile and had no sense?

"So, do I, and quite effectively, but you don't see me running off into a dangerous situation without backup."

"I asked you to come with me today."

"Only because I was there, and I hardly classify this as a dangerous situation." He smiled and patted her arm. "It's only because we care."

"Hog wash." They'd always treated her that way. Maybe she needed to get used to their archaic ideas, do what she would do, and continue on as they had been. A good plan, except Drew was pulling away from her.

She turned onto a dirt driveway in front of a wooden shingled house with a porch that stretched across the front. She hadn't turned off the engine before Mrs. Richards stepped onto the porch.

"Figured you'd show up." She grinned. "I've put the coffee on."

"Thank you. We're kind of hoping the truck will go by while we're here."

"Since he ain't been by this morning, he should…" she glanced at her watch, "be by in about ten minutes. Regular as a baby needing a diaper change, that one."

Inside, Linn shook Lincoln's hand. "Have you been a big help here?"

He nodded. "I take out the trash and help with the dishes. When can I go home? Where is my mommy and Kamal?"

"You'll be with them real soon, okay?" She gave him a quick hug. "I'm working as hard as I can to make that happen. Your brother is a big help, just like you."

She straightened as a dark Ford 150 with a broken taillight passed the house at a snail's pace.

~

Drew waited twenty minutes before Martin Williams came through the visitation doors. "Thank you for meeting with me."

"Sorry I'm late. You came during shower time." The big man sat across from him and folded his hands on the table. He nodded at them. "No more cuffs when I have visitors. I'm a reformed man. Found Jesus last week."

"Congratulations." Drew had heard it before. Men find Christianity, get a few perks, then once out of prison go back to their old ways. For Kamal's sake, he hopes Martin is a changed man. "Glad to hear it, since I need your help."

"I'm not going to like this, am I?"

Drew grinned. "Hopefully, it won't be too painful." He sobered. "We got boys dying. Three boys were picked up by who we believe were the Indigos over a week ago. No one has seen hide nor hair until we found one of them dead yesterday. We're wondering whether these boys are some kind of initiation. Are they taken to see whether someone else has the guts to kill him or to test the boys themselves?"

"Could be either, but I'm leaning toward the boys are killed if they don't accomplish some task." He leaned closer. "I don't know a whole lot about the Indigos since I've been locked up, but they're real bad news. If they want Upton Falls, they'll get it."

Not if Drew had anything to say about it. "They've never come across the law enforcement here. I guess you heard your wife is in jail."

"Yeah, but not for much longer. Where's my boy?"

"Protective custody."

"Kamal?"

"He's infiltrated Devonne's group as our informant." Drew prepared himself for an attack by slowly scooting his chair back and getting to his feet.

"Sit down." Martin made a disgusted sound in his throat. "I ain't going to risk my little bit of freedom by tackling your sorry white ass to the ground. Who's idea was it? I bet it was him, wasn't it?"

"You stepson is very persuasive. Said he was going to anyway and we couldn't stop him."

The other man laughed. "That's my boy. He might not be my biological son, but he's just like me, without having to go through all those bad years. He'll do what's right."

"What he's doing is dangerous. We can't ask too much of him. That's why I'm here talking to you."

Martin straightened. "Ain't a lot more I can tell you. Most likely, the boys were told to rob someone, beat someone up, maybe even shoot. If they refuse, they're killed as an example."

Drew scratched his chin. "Any word on the streets as to where the Indigos boss holds up?"

"He'll be in the nicest place he can find not too far from the hub of things." Martin crossed his arms. "Yep. He'll be holed up in luxury while his minions do his dirty work. More boys will die, Chief. The three gangs will try to off each other until only one remains. Boys will deflect. Things will get ugly. Your town is facing Armageddon if you don't stop this gang."

"I have every intention of stopping them." He thrust out his hand. "Thank you."

Martin stared at it for a minute, then returned the shake. "Stay safe. Keep my boys safe."

"At the expense of my life."

~

Kamal had gone home the night before and thrown up his supper. Now, he stood on trembling legs waiting for his father to sit at the desk he stood in front of.

Had Antonio told him that Kamal hesitated? That he'd closed his eyes. God, don't let him have misaimed and killed the man.

Heavy footsteps behind him announced his uncle's arrival. Kamal kept his gaze forward studying the map of the city on the wall and three different colored pins stuck into the map. He took mental snapshots, knowing there was valuable information in those pins.

Devonne sat, the leather of his chair squeaking under his weight. He heaved a sigh and stared at Kamal. "Well, you did do what I told you to do. You shot the man. Since I didn't order you to kill him, and he still breathes, I'll chalk it up to inexperience."

Kamal's gaze flicked to him. "It's always a kill?"

"Unless I specify otherwise." He steepled his fingers under his chin. "But, I know you don't have the heart for it yet. You need more time. So, I'll respect that. As long as you show me the respect I deserve, we'll get along real fine. Now, get on to school. You're going to be late."

Again. Which meant he'd be in detention for a few days. Oh, well. That would only add to his bad boy image.

The detective and the chief must have seen the video footage by now. He hoped they wouldn't believe he'd done that willingly.

Half an hour later, he marched into the school and was informed by the assistant principal to report to in-school suspension for the next three days. His shoulders slumped as he trudged to the room at the very end of the high school hallway.

The teacher in there barely looked up. "Have a seat. Rules are on the board. Break those rules, spend more time in here."

He groaned and put his forehead on his desk to wait until someone brought him his schoolwork for the day. A wadded piece of paper pelted him in the head.

He narrowed his eyes at a boy sitting one row and one desk back.

"Dude, you've got guts," he whispered. "You robbed a convenience store last night on Greenback turf. Wow. You must have a death wish."

Since they weren't allowed to wear the colors of the gangs making trouble in Upton Falls, Kamal had to assume the other kid was a Greenback. Great. It was going to be a long three days. Not to mention the target on his back got five times bigger.

"Yeah," the other kid said louder. "Ain't many that would do something that stupid."

"No talking," the teacher said. "Leave Kamal alone and focus on the work in front of you.

"Oh, I will. The real work starts after school." The kid laughed.

Kamal got through the day because the teacher never let him out of her sight. The room even had its own bathroom.

After school, Kamal bolted from the room, the other kid on his heels. Kamal was faster, zig-zagging through other students like a wide receiver. Ignoring shouts of no running in the halls, he slammed open the doors and raced across the parking lot. He dove into his car and sped from the parking lot, leaving the other kid standing in the parking lot.

Devonne had to have known of the repercussions of the job he'd ordered Kamal to do. He'd basically signed their death warrant. Why would he want his own son killed?

# Chapter Thirteen

Linn bolted from the house, Steve on her heels. As the truck turned the corner, she slammed her jeep into gear and gave chase.

"This is what I'm talking about." Steve glared as he fastened his seatbelt. "You didn't consult your partner. You automatically gave chase."

"There wasn't time to have a discussion." She increased their speed. "Would you have stayed at the house or gone after the truck?"

"Gone after the truck, but I would have at least given you a signal. If I had been in another room, would you have called for me before taking off?"

"Of course." She rolled her eyes. She would have called out his name, but she wouldn't have waited more than a second for him to respond. Later, when things slowed down, she'd think long and hard about whether or not the men in her life really had something to worry about or whether they were simply overprotective because of her encounter with

The Photographer last year.

Steve's phone buzzed. He glanced at the screen. "The chief wants us back in the office to look at some store security footage."

"Text him that we're in pursuit of a suspicious person and will be in when we're finished." Drew shouldn't have a problem with that since Linn had Steve with her.

The truck must have spotted them because it increased its speed. Linn followed suit just to the point where she bordered on going too fast around the mountain roads. "We're losing him."

"Stay on his tail the best you can." Steve set his handgun on the dash.

"You expecting some shooting?" She raised a brow.

"Always be prepared. You focus on driving so we don't crash, I'll take care of anything that pops up."

That suited her fine. She concentrated on taking the corners fast, grateful for no oncoming traffic. Occasionally, she'd spot the truck as it rounded another corner and prayed there weren't any roads it could shoot down where she'd lose it.

She lost it. "Tell me you got the license plate."

"Most of it. The tech guy should be able to figure it out."

They weren't close to stopping the violence than they were when the gangs arrived in town. Things were escalating to Defcon 4 faster than law enforcement could keep up. "Tell Drew we're on our way."

After a quick stop back at Mrs. Richards to let her know they'd failed to catch up to the truck and leaving her with a warning to keep Lincoln out of sight, Linn headed back into town. If the truck came by every day, then someone suspected the boy to be in that house. She needed to consider moving him to another safe location. Problem was, she didn't know of anyone she trusted more than Mrs. Richards.

They met Drew in the conference room where he had a laptop set up. The grave expression on his face alerted her to the fact she wouldn't like what she would see on the footage.

He turned the screen to face them.

Kamal didn't try to hide his face. Neither did the other boy with him.

Linn flinched when the shot rang out and the clerk fell.

"He shot someone." Steve peered closer.

"Look." Linn rewound. "He closed his eyes and aimed low. It's clear the other boy is egging him on. Kamal did this reluctantly."

"But he did pull the trigger," Drew said.

She stared open-mouthed for a second. "He's undercover. Sometimes they do the least of what is required in order to keep their cover. Surely, you don't think he *wanted* to pull the trigger?"

"I'd like to think not."

"That store is on Greenback turf," Lydia said, entering the room. "Kamal will be targeted. So will the other boy."

"Why put his own son in danger?" Steve glanced around the group.

"That's what I'd like for you to find out. Take Rodriguez with you. I want Linn to question the clerk in the hospital."

"What are you going to be doing?" More secrets?

He faced her. "Digging into the leader of the Indigos."

The sharp look in his eyes left her feeling pushed aside. Normally, they collaborated on every aspect of a case. Now, she felt excluded. Pain ripped at her heart. "I'll head to the hospital now." Without another glance in his direction, she left the room.

She blinked back tears as she drove to the hospital. Something had gone horribly wrong between her and Drew, and she had no idea how to fix…whatever it was.

A volunteer pointed her to the correct room as soon as she showed her identification at the hospital. Linn rapped on the patient's door and entered when told to do so. She identified herself again. "Mind if I ask you a few questions?"

"Not at all." The man sat up straighter in his bed.

"What can you tell me about last night?" She stood at the foot of the bed.

"Two young men came in, both armed. The one who shot me ordered me to empty the register. I did, so I'm not sure why he shot me other than the fact the other one kept shouting in his face to do so or he'd have to shoot him. The boy who pulled the trigger, did not want to, I'm pretty positive about that."

Which eased some of Linn's worry. "Did he say anything?"

"Not much. The other boy did most of the talking. This one looked terrified. Clearly out of his element."

"Thank you." Linn stepped back into the hall. She really needed to pay a visit to Devonne.

~

The receptionist alerted them to a body found in the shallows of the lake.

Steve nodded. "We'll check that out before digging into why Kamal was sent to someone else's turf."

"Okay. Stay safe, everyone." Drew started to brush past

them.

"Do you have a second, Chief?" Steve motioned for Lydia to go ahead of him.

"A short one. What's up?"

"It's probably none of my business, other than the fact that a muddled mind is dangerous under these circumstances." He braced himself for some backlash. "Is everything okay with you and Linn?"

Drew stared at him for so long, Steve knew without a doubt that he had overstepped his bounds. "I'm sorry. None of my business." He turned to go.

"It's alright. I'm keeping my distance during this case for the exact reason you stated. Linn scares me to death with her foolish bravery, something I also admire. I can't let myself dwell on the danger of her being…Linn. Let's get this case solved quickly so life gets back to normal, whatever normal is."

"Amen to that." Steve completely understood Drew's feelings. While he no longer loved Linn with a romantic love as he once had, he did love her and would be devastated to lose his partner and friend. He glanced to where Lydia waited. Now, he found himself worrying about another. "I guess worrying is part of this job."

"When you work with loved ones, it is. Good luck today." Drew clapped him on the shoulder and marched to his office.

Steve joined Lydia at the front door. "Ready?"

"I'm never ready to see a dead body."

Neither was he.

Twenty minutes later, he stared at the body of the boy in security video. He'd been shot execution style. He exhaled heavily, feeling the weight of the world on his shoulders. Too much death.

"Maybe I'm not cut out for this." Lydia stared at the body. "I thought we'd have to soothe ruffled feathers, maybe lock up a drunk or two. I never dreamed I'd be in the middle of a gang war staring at the body of a dead kid every day." She blinked rapidly and looked away.

He put a hand on his shoulder, then jerked back as if burned. "That's the type of emotion that makes you a good police officer. You never get used to this, Lydia. Not if you have a heart. You'll find yourself more driven, more empathetic."

She turned reddened eyes on him. "Maybe I don't want that." She took a deep breath. "I'll go get the crime scene tape."

He wanted to reassure her, comfort her, but simply touching her had drug out emotions he wasn't ready to experience again. If he worried about her now, how much more would he if he allowed his emotions to move forward? Cases like the one they dealt with didn't allow for romantic entanglement. Not with a high body count. So far, they'd been lucky that no one had targeted one of Upton Falls's law enforcement.

He helped her secure the scene, then placed the call to the chief and the ME. Nothing to do now but wait since there were no people around to question. He glanced at the trees surrounding the lake.

"What is it?" Lydia asked, following his gaze.

"On a nice day like this, this path is usually full of joggers and hikers. Who found the body and where are they?"

"Anonymous call."

Dread seized Steve's heart. A twig snapped behind him. He tackled Lydia to the ground as a shot rang out.

When something crashed through the brush, he lunged to his feet and withdrew his weapon. "Come on." He charged into the trees, Lydia on his heals.

The shooter made as much noise as a bull roaring through the trees. Steve caught a flash of green, then nothing as the shooter got ahead of them. There. The shooter had circled around to their right.

"He's headed for the lake." Lydia turned and darted that way. "He must have a boat."

Steve shoved a low-hanging branch out of his way and burst from the trees.

A teenage boy sprinted along the shoreline away from the body. He cast a surly look over his shoulder and aimed the gun in his hand. His shot went wild.

"Stop!" Steve raised his weapon. "Don't make me shoot you." Please. He'd never get over shooting a kid, even an armed one.

Lydia didn't seem anymore inclined to fire than he did. Her gun hand hung at her side.

Crap. Steve fired into the air.

The boy froze, hands over his head and slowly turned to face them. "What kind of a cop shoots at a kid?"

"Lucky for you, I shot over your head. Toss the gun toward that rock."

The boy did as told.

"You shoot that boy back there?"

"No. I found him like that. I'm the one who called it in."

"Then why run from the scene?" Steve lowered his gun

and motioned for Lydia to retrieve the boy's weapon. "We can find out if it's been fired recently."

"I know. Same as you can find out the bullet won't match. Can I put my hands down now?"

"No. Officer Rodriguez and I found you near a recently murdered kid. Then, you run. You shot at us. That right there is reason enough for me to lock you up. If you're so innocent, why shoot at us?"

"To give me time to get away." He hung his head. "I didn't aim to hit. You're still breathing, ain't you?"

"If you didn't shoot the victim, who did?"

"Someone who wants you to think it's the Greenbacks. That kid belonged to the Royals. You dig deep enough, you'll find out that an Indigo killed him."

"This isn't retaliation for him being one of those who knocked over the convenience store?"

He shook his head. "No, they want to pin Devonne's kid on that one."

Steve's blood chilled. Kamal was in a lot of trouble.

# Chapter Fourteen

Linn swallowed past a suddenly dry throat. "He actually said the Indigos are targeting Kamal?"

"Pretty much." Steve checked the ammo in his gun.

"We need to talk to Devonne. Kamal needs to go into protective custody." She grabbed her coat.

"I doubt we'll get close enough to speak to the man, but alright." Steve followed her to her jeep. "Try not to be confrontational."

"Me?" She put a hand to her chest.

"Don't play innocent. I'm always the good cop when we're together."

She laughed, knowing he stated the truth. "I'll behave." It wouldn't benefit anyone for her to rile Devonne. Least of all his nephew.

She drove them to the hotel Devonne had taken over, pitying the owner of the place. It had once been a place where couples went to get away for the night in a nice room with a wonderful restaurant. Now, it housed one of the worst crime lords and his men.

"No time like the present." She shoved her door open, making sure her weapon was visible and accessible.

"Already playing the bad cop," Steve said.

She covered her gun with the hem of her jacket. "Habit."

Shoulder-to-shoulder, they approached the double glass doors where a young man stood watching them approach. Linn started to flash her badge, but the man waved it away.

"We know who you are. State your business."

"We're here to speak to Devonne about his nephew." She squared her shoulders.

"Not sure he has the time." He studied his fingernails.

"We won't know unless you ask him, will we?" She forced the question through gritted teeth.

Without sparing her a glance, he opened the door. "Check in at the desk."

Shooting Steve a glance, she approached the teenager at the desk. "We're here to see Devonne."

"Sign the book and leave your weapons." His gaze clashed with hers. "You aren't allowed to go further without leaving them. They'll be here when you come back down."

"Play nice," Steve whispered, setting his service revolver on the desk.

Disarming herself went against every bone in her body. Keeping her gaze locked with the teen behind the desk, she set her gun next to Steve's.

"Top floor." The boy arched a brow.

"Thanks." Linn marched to the elevator, Steve right behind her.

Three minutes later, they faced another man, this one

outside a door, Linn assumed kept Devonne from public view. "Detectives MacFarland and Chavez here to speak to Devonne."

"I'll see if he's available." He stepped into the room, returning a few seconds later. He patted them down, then motioned them inside.

Devonne sat in a black leather chair, a drink in his hand. "Welcome. Want something to drink?" He snapped his fingers and a scantily dressed woman rushed from the hall.

"No, thank you." Linn breathed deep through her nose. "Why did you put a target on your nephew's back? The Greenbacks are gunning for him now."

He laughed. "Do you always get straight to the point?"

"Life is too short to do otherwise." Especially lately.

"Kamal needs to learn to survive out there. This won't be the only time someone goes after him. He needs to learn how to handle these types of situations." He leaned forward and set his glass on the coffee table.

"Where is he now?"

"He'd best be at school." He propped his feet on the table, crossing them at the ankles. "Where did you stash the other boy?"

"That's classified information."

"I'm not going to hurt my son's brother. He might as well join his brother in the family business."

Linn frowned. "He's only seven."

"There are jobs a child that age can do."

The man was despicable. "Let's stay focused on Kamal for now. We'd like to put him in protective custody."

"That would show weakness to the others." He crossed his arms. "My nephew will be fine, Detective."

Being nice wasn't easy. Heat rose up her neck.

Steve gave a slight shake of his head. "Sir, we can arrest him for robbing the convenience store and shooting the clerk."

"Think that would keep him safe?" He laughed. "Do what you must. Jail will toughen him up." He got to his feet. "Now, if you're finished, I have work to do." He picked up his cell phone from the coffee table. Still smiling, he ordered that Kamal take off because the cops were coming to arrest him.

Linn narrowed her eyes, biting her tongue not to tell the idiot what she thought of him. Kamal might pretend to run, might even go into hiding for a few days. She'd take it. Even hiding for a few days could make a difference.

She turned and marched from the man's room. Once in the elevator, she faced Steve. "He doesn't care anything at all for his son."

"He probably does in his own way. He's grooming Kamal to someday take his place." He pressed the button for the ground floor.

"We are nowhere close to shutting down these gangs. More kids are going to die. One of them might be Kamal." The thought tore at her heart despite the fact she'd only been around him for minutes at a time.

~

Arrest him? Why would Detective MacFarland want him locked up? They needed him.

Kamal drove out of town, the backseat holding bags of groceries and a case of bottled water. He could hold up in a vacant barn for a day or two, but no longer. He only followed his uncle's order to keep things "real".

Boredom set in before nightfall. Using his burner phone, he called the detective. "Why'd my uncle send me away?"

"To keep us from arresting you or putting you in protective custody. He's admitted to putting you directly in danger. Wants to see how you handle things."

He closed his eyes and leaned his head against the rough wood of the barn wall. "I figured that out on my own. How do I handle this without killing someone? I'm not able to get the info on Devonne that you want. I haven't done a very good job by y'all."

"You're doing great. I'd rather keep you alive than worry about you obtaining information. Are you somewhere safe?"

"I doubt anyone would expect me to be living in a barn that's ready to fall down." He sighed. "How is Lincoln?"

"Being taken care of."

"Are y'all close to shutting this down?"

"I'm sorry to say that we are not. We've not laid eyes on a single Indigo unless they're wearing other colors."

He'd bet that's what they're doing. "I know most of the Greenbacks from school. If they didn't all want me dead, I could see whether there were any new faces."

"I appreciate that, but not at this time. You lay low for a few days. I'll be in touch." She hung up, leaving him feeling lonelier than he could ever recall feeling.

He bent his knees, wrapped his arms around them, and cried for the first time in a very long time. When he felt he had no more tears to shed, he opened a water bottle, set it on the ground next to his sleeping bag, and curled up to go to sleep as a couple of rats nosed around his grocery bags.

~

Steve decided to cruise the street where the Royals and the Greenbacks roamed. He slowed, spotting a woman who looked like…it was Lydia. He leaned forward, eyes peeled. She seemed deep in a conversation with several of the Greenbacks.

On the other side of the street, the Royals watched.

How could a rookie cop feel comfortable enough to converse with a dangerous gang? They knew she was a cop. Did this have anything to do with her grandfather's past?

She turned, her eyes widening when she spotted Steve.

He stopped next to the curb and rolled down the window. "Officer."

"Detective."

"I didn't expect to see you here."

"Thought I'd ask some questions before heading home."

"Out of uniform?" It didn't feel right to him. "Obviously, you don't believe yourself to be in any danger."

"No, these boys know my grandfather. He may not be in organized crime anymore, but he's still respected on the streets." She leaned on the door. "You think I'm up to no good." A shadow flickered across her eyes. "I'm not my grandfather, but I'm not against using his name to get information."

"Did you?" He tilted his head.

"Yep. Meet me at the coffee shop on Main." She slapped the doorframe before heading to her car.

Knowing she'd found out something did little to soothe his annoyance at the fact she'd questioned dangerous gang members alone. He did a U-turn in the street and headed for the other side of town. He waited inside for fifteen minutes before Lydia arrived.

"Sorry." She settled into a seat across from him. "Had to break up a scuffle between two boys."

"Opposing gang members?"

She nodded. "Same ones from the restaurant over the same girl."

"What do you want to drink?" Steve stood.

"Pomegranate green tea." She smiled. "Thanks."

He ordered her drink and a plain black coffee for himself. While he waited, he watched from across the room as Lydia scrolled through her phone. Maybe her grandfather was still respected in the crime world, but that didn't mean Lydia could do whatever she wanted without being in danger. In fact, someone might have something to prove to her family and kill her to make a point. Or, worse, Lydia decided to follow in her grandfather's footsteps using law enforcement as a cover.

When had he grown so cynical? When Queen Coral, a woman he thought he could love, tried to kill him. When Linn chose Drew. Romance came hard for him. He knew he shouldn't have let his guard down and looked at Lydia as a woman instead of a cop.

A streetlight shined on her dark head highlighting strands of copper. She glanced outside, giving him a perfect view of her profile.

"Sir? Your drinks are ready." The barista grinned. "I've called your name three times."

"My apologies." He took the drinks and returned to the table. Once seated, he asked, "What's your news?"

She tilted her head. "Why are you surly?"

No need to lie. "I think you're hiding something from me. Something about your family."

She rolled her eyes. "I assure you that I am not. The chief trusts me, why can't you?"

"Trust doesn't come easy."

She gave a one-shoulder shrug. "The Indigos are wearing opposing colors to pit the gangs against each other."

"Which we suspected." He sipped his coffee, wincing as the scalding liquid burned his lip.

"Now confirmed." She took a drag on her straw. "Trust me, Steve. I like you. You're a super guy and a great detective. Even though my family left the gang life, I can still use the name to get me in places you and the others can't go. I chose not to wear my uniform so no one felt intimidated. Let's use what we can."

He tore his gaze from her lips wrapped around the straw. Poor besotted fool. "Have you discussed this with the chief?"

"Not yet. I'll fill him in tomorrow."

"I wouldn't want to be on the lecture end you'll be on tomorrow. He likes things done by the book, especially with the rookies."

Another shrug. "Detective MacFarland gets things done by going with her gut. That's all I did."

"You are not a detective."

She grinned. "Someday, I will be. Maybe you and I will be partners. We make a great team."

God help him. They were thrown together enough as it was. He made a noncommittal sound and focused on his coffee.

"I know where the Indigos are staying," she whispered. "At least a strong suspicion."

"Really? Where?" This would be a game changer.

She nodded. "They're staying on a farm about twenty miles from here. My informant told me they purchased the land and buildings and have started building an empire."

"Do we know where exactly?"

"No, but I bet we can find out by using a chopper or a drone." She wiggled her eyebrows. "I told you I had information."

"Why not lead with the good?" He grinned. "When you talk to the chief, tell him about the farm first. It'll soften him up."

"Will do." She got up and thanked him for the tea, then strolled out the door.

Steve stood and headed for the door.

A car engine revved.

Headlights outlined Lydia's body seconds before she dove to the sidewalk.

Somebody screamed.

# Chapter Fifteen

Steve bolted from the coffee shop and knelt next to Lydia. She lay crumpled against the brick wall of the building. A purple knot rose on her forehead, contrasting with the red of scraped skin. He cupped her cheek. "Open your eyes, sweetheart."

He glanced up as the roar of motorcycles filled the street. The bikers who had promised to help run the gangs out of town gave chase to the car which had almost struck Lydia.

"Come on, Lydia, open your eyes." He patted her cheek with one hand while fishing for his cell phone with the other.

"I've called for an ambulance," the barista said. "Is she dead?"

"No." Thank God. But she was unresponsive. "Lydia?" He bent low over her face.

Her eyelids fluttered open. "Were you going to wake me with a kiss?" She smiled, then frowned. "Ow."

"Where does it hurt?" He ran his hands up and down her

body.

"As much as I'd like to explore you doing that a bit further, this isn't the place." A smile teased at her lips. "Help me sit up. Other than some bruises I know I'll have, it's my head that aches."

His face flushed. "I wasn't being, uh, intimate with you."

"In public? I think not."

He helped her sit as an ambulance blocked the cars in front of the shop.

"Who tried to run me over?" Her gaze searched his face.

"I don't know, but I suspect it had to do with your talking to the Greenbacks. Our biker friends took off after the car. Hopefully, they'll catch the driver." He stepped back as the paramedics took over and stared in the direction the motorcycles had gone.

He felt torn between going to the hospital with Lydia and giving chase himself. With a heavy sigh, he watched as the paramedics helped her into the ambulance. Hospital it would be. He turned to the barista. "If the bikers return, tell them to come to the hospital to speak with me."

"Yes, sir."

Steve hopped in his car and followed the ambulance. He continued to do so into the hospital and into the curtained alcove they wheeled Lydia into and sat in the only vacant plastic chair. His gaze focused on the pale face of Lydia. She could have been killed.

"Don't look so worried." She stretched out her hand. "I'm going to be fine. It's sweet to know you don't dislike me as much as I thought."

"Why would you think that?" He jerked, then took her

hand. "I'm sorry if I gave you that impression." Was he really such a hard nose?

"You're awfully gruff at times, Detective." She lay her head back and closed her eyes. "But, I might be too if I discovered my twin was a serial killer." She opened one eye. "You aren't the only one who reads files. Besides, I followed that case very carefully. I'd like to take down someone like your brother during my career."

A laugh escaped him. "You really did hit your head."

"Detective." A nurse poked her head around the curtain. "There are several rough looking gentlemen here to see you."

"I'll be back." He pulled his hand free of Lydia's, feeling as if he'd lost something, and hurried to the waiting room.

Two of the bikers held the arms of a teenager who sported a black eye and several scrapes of his own. The biggest of the two raised his hand. "Before you go thinking we beat up a kid, let me tell you that he got all this trying to run and fell in a ditch." They released the boy, who tried to run, only to find his path blocked by the two men.

"Thanks, guys. I'll take it from here." Steve removed a pair of handcuffs from his belt and cuffed the boy before leading him back toward Lydia's room. Seeing the alcove next to her vacant, he secured the boy to the bed. "I'll question you later. Nurse, could you check him out, please?"

She nodded.

Steve rejoined Lydia. "The driver of the car who tried to run you down is cuffed to the bed in the other examination room. Figured you might want to be there when I question him."

"Absolutely." She sat up. "I've got nothing more serious than a concussion. Doctor is filling out my release papers. He can give them to me in the other room same as here."

He placed his hand on the small of her back. The warmth of her skin reached him through the thin tee shirt she wore. He swallowed a sigh, knowing his heart had betrayed him. He hadn't realized it until he'd seen her lying on the sidewalk.

"Hey." Lydia grinned real big and stood in front of the boy who hung his head. "I know you, Willy. Everyone thinks you're dead."

Willy? "Why did you try to run over Officer Rodriguez?" Steve crossed his arms.

"If I didn't, they'd kill me same as they did Carl." Tears ran down his cheeks. "I had to prove my loyalty. If you lock me up, I'm as good as dead."

"We'll put you in protective custody. Your mother is worried sick, son. I'll get a phone so you can call her." He uncuffed him from the bed and led him to the nurse's station.

~

The next morning, Linn and Drew listened as Steve filled them in on the events of the previous night. At least one boy's life had been saved. "How's Lydia?"

"Fine, but trying to get her to stay home for a couple of days as the doctor ordered is like holding down a rabid dog." Steve poured creamer into his coffee. "What's on the agenda for today?"

"I want you and Linn to check out the alleged home of the Indigos." Drew glanced from Steve to Linn. "Do not engage without backup. You call me once you've confirmed that's where they are."

"Okay." Linn would follow his order unless they had to move or lose their chance of arrest.

"I mean it, Linn." He set his jaw.

"I said okay." She shoved her arm through the sleeve of her jacket and slid her weapon into its holster. "I will use discretion."

"That isn't what I said."

She pretended not to hear him, planted a quick kiss on his lips, and marched from the building. "Anyone up in the air yet?"

Steve opened the passenger side door to the jeep. "Chopper will be up in five."

"We'll be ready to go where they send us." She climbed into the driver's seat and started the engine. They could have five minutes to wait or half an hour. "Want to grab something to eat? I haven't had breakfast."

"Sure. A breakfast burrito sounds good." He continued to stare.

"What?"

"I'm going to do my best to make sure you follow the chief's orders."

"Knock yourself out." She chuckled and drove toward a Mexican food truck that served great breakfast burritos.

The radio in the car crackled as they sat and ate breakfast. "I think I found the farm." The pilot gave directions. "Want me to keep circling?"

"No, you'll scare them off." Linn wadded up the wrapper and stuffed it in the jeep's console. "Let's go catch some crooks."

Half an hour later, she parked at the end of a dirt road.

They'd have to go the rest of the way on foot.

"Remember. We're only here to clarify that this is where they're holed up." Steve shot her a stern look.

"Understood." She really wished the two men in her life would let her do her job. She had good instincts, trusted her gut feeling during dangerous situations. Why treat her as if she didn't have a level head on her shoulders?

The trudged through the woods about the length of a football field before she started to hear voices and the sound of a drill. She slowed, parting the low-hanging branches of an oak tree.

Men swarmed from a sprawling two-story farmhouse. A traditional-style barn dominated the cleared land. Construction of another building that looked similar to an old-fashioned bunkhouse stood half complete. No one wore the Indigo color.

"Do you think it's the Indigos?" She whispered.

"Has to be. I guess they only wear their color when they're in town."

"Let's get closer. I want to see who the leader is." She took a step forward.

Steve shot out his arm and stopped her. "There."

A tall man with dreads hanging over his shoulders stepped from the house. He stood on the porch and surveyed the work going on around him. A few seconds later, the most exotic woman Linn had ever seen joined him. Ebony skin shiny with oil, almond shaped eyes, high cheekbones…why would such a beautiful woman be involved with a gang lord? She belonged in the movies, not here.

The man barked something at her, his Jamaican accent heavy. She scurried back into the house.

"Guess he doesn't want his men watching her," Steve said. "Come on. We've seen what we came to see." He tapped her shoulder.

It took every bit of strength to pull back and follow Steve back to the car. But, they were grossly outnumbered and would have no chance in a gunfight.

"The chief would be proud." Steve grinned, getting back into the jeep.

"Ha ha." She backed from the road and back to blacktop. "We didn't see the colors, but the accent is official enough for me. Guess Drew will call in the swat team?"

"Our little force isn't big enough to take them down. We'll definitely need help."

She nodded. "Get rid of the Indigos, then the other two. Restore peace to Upton Falls."

Sounded a lot easier than it would be. There'd be a war before all was said and done, and their little law enforcement would be smack dab in the middle of it all. Which meant Drew would be in the middle.

Her hands tightened on the wheel. That's why she plunged headfirst into danger. This needed to end before it got to the point where the man she loved could die again. He might not be able to be resuscitated the next time. She couldn't live without him by her side.

"What's wrong? We accomplished something today." Steve tilted his head.

"Oh, nothing. Wishing it to all go away. There're two brothers who need to be reunited." If they survived. "And a wedding to plan." She cut him a sideways glance. "How are you and Lydia getting along?" She wiggled her eyebrows.

"Fine." Furrows cut across his forehead. "We work

together, Linn. That's all."

She laughed. "Sure. Say it often enough and you might come to believe your words."

"I swore off romance, remember?"

"Doesn't mean it swore off you." She really hoped he could find happiness with a good woman. Her partner deserved love and a family.

Back at the office, they headed straight for Drew's office and told him what they'd found.

"It definitely looks as if they plan on sticking around," Linn said. "Lots of building, lots of men."

"How many?" He asked.

"We didn't get a headcount," Steve answered, "but I'm guessing at least twenty. Mostly teens and men in their twenties. I'd say the man we believe to be the leader to be in his late twenties. Only saw one woman, no children."

Linn nodded. "Do you think we need to clear out the homeless park? Make sure no more teens are paying them visits? The Indigos could be about ready to recruit again."

"We'd be wasting our time." Drew tapped a pen on his desk. "They'd leave and be right back by dark. What we need is manpower. A couple of officers to patrol the area. I'll contact Little Rock to see about borrowing some officers and get the Swat team ready. We need to swarm that farm and bring this group down."

# Chapter Sixteen

Linn entered the police department early the next morning. The only person there before her was their receptionist, Lucy.

"Thank God." Lucy hung up the phone. "Just got a call in about a woman lying dead in a ditch. Here's the address." She handed Linn a slip of paper.

She recognized the address as the neighborhood where Kamal's home was. "I'll take care of it. Let the chief know when he arrives." She turned and rushed back to her vehicle. Please don't be Kamal's mother. The boy had been through enough in his life.

A crowd had gathered near the Williams home. Linn parked and marched toward the scene. Spectators parted as if she were Moses parting the red sea.

Tanisha Williams lay half on the sidewalk, half in the grass. No bullet wounds that she could see. Linn bent and checked for a pulse. Weak, but there. She smoothed back the woman's hair. "Someone call an ambulance. Now."

The woman's face had been beaten to the point she most likely had a broken jaw. Both eyes were swelled shut. Her lip bled from a split. Linn doubted she was meant to still be breathing.

But who? Devonne or one of the others? And why a woman who had only recently been released from jail? She straightened.

"Anyone see or hear anything?" Her gaze searched the crowd.

Heads shook.

Someone had to have seen something. A woman wasn't beaten without sound, unless she'd been beaten somewhere else and dumped here.

Linn searched the ground for clues, frowning at all the signs of trampled ground from looky-lous. Had no one thought to help Tanisha?

Two sedans traveling in opposite directions slowed. Linn's gaze met the dark eyes of one of the drivers. The teen lifted an assault rifle, then riddled the other vehicle with bullets.

"Get down!" Linn dove to the ground as the teen then turned the weapon on the crowd.

Screams filled the air. Bullets shattered the morning. Tires squealed as the shooters sped away. Then, all fell quiet except for whimpering and cries of pain.

Linn got to her feet, taking assessment of any possible injuries to herself. She hadn't been hit. Other than a hole in the knee of her pants and a scrape, she'd gotten off lucky. It wasn't until she bent to check on Tanisha again that she noticed the pain radiating up her left arm. A quick glance revealed a bullet graze. Not as unscathed as she'd hoped.

Still, she'd live.

Sirens wailed in the distance. Good. She'd have help with the wounded.

She made her rounds, doing her best to determine those in most need of medical attention. Three needed no attention at all. Her heart ached at the show of violence, the lack of care regarding human life.

She called for an additional ambulance, then separated the uninjured from the injured. "Go home. Hug your loved ones."

"We're in the middle of a turf war, ain't we?" An old man shook his head, leaning heavily on a simple aluminum cane.

"I'm afraid so, sir."

He gave a weary nod. "It ain't safe to step outside in the daytime or the nighttime. Come soon, Lord Jesus." He shuffled away, still shaking his head.

Movement from the side of the house caught her eye. She spun to see Kamal watching. She motioned for him to stay where he was. Things were too dangerous for him to be out in the open. It was no coincidence that the shooting took place in front of his house.

She moved to check on those in the car. Three teens all still alive, thankfully. "Can you speak?"

"Yeah." The driver clutched his leg.

"Greenback?"

He nodded.

"The other car?"

"Indigo. It was a trap. We were told to come here to get Kamal." He winced, closing his eyes.

"To kill him, you mean?"

"As a sign to Devonne to back down."

Linn stared at the other two boys. "You do know that you and the Royals are being pitted against each other, right? That it's the Indigos stirring things up?"

"Yeah, but Devonne is in this deeper than you know." The driver opened his eyes. "Word on the street is that he's been bought."

Linn stiffened. "Who's the source?"

"If I tell you that, the guy is dead. Look, lady. We need help here. I'm going to bleed out."

"No, you're not." She gave what she hoped was a reassuring smile. "You three got lucky."

The ambulance pulled up and she turned to direct them to the more seriously wounded, before searching for Kamal. She found him behind a garden shed with a sagging roof and no door.

"It's too dangerous for you to be here," she said.

"I heard my mom was dead."

"Not yet, but she's been beat up real bad." She tilted his head. "Any idea who?"

"No, but I'll be asking around."

"Could it be Devonne?" She wanted to tell him what the Greenbacks had told her, but held off. The last thing she needed was for him to run off in a fit of rage to confront his uncle.

"Maybe." He shrugged. "But why? He's told me before that he loves her."

"She's still married to Martin, correct? Maybe he's questioning her loyalty."

His eyes widened. "That doesn't make sense. Martin gets out of prison soon. Why beat up the woman he plans on coming home to. Mom needs him to get her clean. He wouldn't order a hit on her."

"Okay. Settle down. I'm only asking." She caught sight of Drew marching toward her, a stormy look on his face.

~

He wanted to wring her neck. His heart dropped at the sight of blood staining through her jacket and slacks. His gaze flicked to Kamal. "I'm taking you in, son. You aren't going to survive the week if I don't."

"Under what pretense?"

"Gang fight." He put two fingers to his lips and let out a piercing whistle.

Steve joined them.

"We're taking Kamal in for his safety. Mind doing the honors? I need to speak to Linn. Take him directly to the station. We can't chance someone getting to him while he waits in the car."

"Sure thing." Steve cuffed the boy, then led him to the squad car.

"You're bleeding." He forced the words through clenched teeth, something he seemed to be doing a lot of lately.

"Just a graze and a scrape. Drew…" she reached out to put a hand on his arm.

He stepped back. "We'll talk later. Right now you need medical attention." He turned and trudged away from her before he said something he'd regret.

When he got to the office and heard about Linn going to check out a call, he'd been irritated. But then hearing about shots fired and several people down, he'd gotten so scared, his chest had hurt. Then, he'd gotten angry about her going on her own.

She'd been doing her job, and he hated it. Living in fear over losing her every day was taking a toll on him. He felt old. He'd been in the same situation when The Photographer had taken her and thought he could deal with loving a woman in law enforcement. Now, he wasn't so sure.

Lydia, in uniform, moved slowly among the wounded.

"You cleared for work?" He asked.

"I've nothing more than a dull headache." She exhaled heavily through her nose. "I did some digging into my family's past while at home yesterday and found out something I think you should know."

"Okay."

"It's common knowledge that Devonne and my grandfather hated each other. What isn't common knowledge is the fact that my grandfather is responsible for the death of Devonne's oldest son."

"Another boy other than Kamal?" This was news.

She nodded. "The death was an accident. A case of mistaken identity." Her gaze locked on his. "Chief, I think Devonne is planning on making sure not one Perez or anyone loyal to them keeps breathing."

"One of the Greenbacks told me that word is that Devonne is working with the Indigos." Linn stepped beside him. "That backs up Lydia's story."

Drew rubbed his chin. How were they going to stop the approaching gang war? The Greenbacks couldn't win against two rival gangs. Innocent people would be caught in the crosshairs.

"Thanks. If you insist on working, then go to the office. Take calls and fill out reports. I don't want you in the field for a few more days. Linn, have a paramedic check you out. I think your arm needs stitches." He marched away, leaving her with a stunned look on her face. He'd spoken to her as someone who worked for him, not as the woman he loved. He dreaded the upcoming talk he planned to have with her.

Linn had been home for a couple of hours before he arrived. He found her curled up on the sofa eating popcorn and watching a comedy sitcom.

"Long day." She smiled.

"Yep." He loosened his tie. "We need to talk."

Alarm flickered across her face as she set the popcorn bowl on the coffee table before turning off the TV.

Rather than sit next to her as he usually did, Drew sat in the chair across from her. He took a deep breath and folded his hands before meeting her gaze. "You're killing me."

She frowned.

"I can't deal with the fact your life is in danger every day."

"I feel the same about you." She leaned forward. "This is our job. Our life. The one we chose."

"I'm not sure I want this life anymore." His eyes burned.

"What are you saying?"

"That one of us has to quit."

"You mean me."

He nodded.

"What would I do, Drew? This is my career." Tears trickled down her face. "You're asking me to choose between my job or you?"

"Yes." He hiked his chin, hating the fact he was asking her to do this out of selfishness. "Maybe not permanently.

Just until we get the gangs out of here."

She lunged to her feet. "That is the most ridiculous thing I've ever heard! How about you take a leave of absence? If you're so worried for my welfare, then stay glued to my side. I won't mind."

"That isn't always possible." He stood and moved toward her, not touching her. To touch her meant to lose his resolve.

"I gave up the FBI job to stay in Upton Falls with you. Can't you do this one thing for me?" His gaze searched her face.

"If I don't?"

"Then I don't know." The words ripped at his heart.

"Sleep on the sofa tonight and figure it out." She stomped away, taking his heart with her.

~

Kamal sat with bowed head, the only occupant in the jail cell. No one had come to tell him about his mother. Did Devonne know he'd been arrested? Would someone come to kill him while he sat in a cage?

What an idiot he'd been to think he could get information from Devonne to give to the authorities? He'd done nothing to help anyone. Whatever information they received came from other sources. Kamal had been useless.

Did Lincoln miss him? What kind of house was he living in? Somewhere that would spoil him to the life he'd have to return to, most likely.

He stood and paced the cell. He had to get out of here and confront his uncle. He pressed his face against the cell door. "Hey! I didn't get my phone call." Devonne would have him out in no time.

# Chapter Seventeen

After a restless night regretting having sent Drew to the sofa, and too proud to bring him back to the room, Linn now sat with Steve across the table from a sullen Martin. Perfect start to what promised to be a rough day.

Her and Drew had gone through so much together in the year they've been together. They'd had their ups and downs, but always came out on top. She really did need to let go. A strong man, a smart man, Drew could take care of himself. Same as she could. Why couldn't he see that she was just as capable as he?

Steve elbowed her. "You with us?"

"Sorry." She gave herself a mental shake. "Martin, we need to know how to bring down your brother."

"Wow. Straight to the point."

"We don't have time to skirt around the issue." She folded her hands on top of the table. "You're about to be released from here. We've taken Kamal into protective custody. We believe that Devonne is working with the

Indigos."

"No way. He'd never work for Trayvon."

"You know the name of the leader?"

"Word gets around." He crossed his arms and leaned back in his chair until the guard ordered the chair flat on the floor. He lowered it with a bang.

"We have a strong reason to believe you're wrong, Mr. Williams."

"Why would he?"

"The long ago feud with Perez."

He frowned. "That's a long time to hold a grudge, even for my brother." He leaned forward, elbows on the table. "You're telling me that my brother will join a rival in order to eradicate another?"

"That's exactly what I'm saying. We need your help. You know Devonne better than anyone." If he refused, she didn't know what their next step would be.

He shook his head. "He'll kill Kamal."

"The boy will most likely die if you don't help us," Steve said. "With your help, he'll at least have a chance. We need to get something on your brother that not even he can get out of."

"He'd have to kill a cop." The big man rubbed both hands down his face.

"Without resorting to that, please." Linn shuddered. "There's already been an attempt on one of our officers. We don't need another."

"He'll go after the man at the top." Martin lowered his voice. "He'll go after the chief. Catch him and prove he was behind the deed."

Use Drew as bait? Absolutely not. She cut a wide eyed

glance at Steve. "There has to be another way."

"I'll confront Devonne."

"No." She put a hand on his arm. She didn't want either of the men she loved to risk their lives. "We'll find another way."

"My brother has enough money to buy his way out of trouble. If he tries to kill a cop, even his money won't save him."

The room started to spin. Her heart fluttered. "We can arrest him on a multitude of things."

"He'll get off." Steve took her hands in his. "Let me do this. Better me than Drew if something goes wrong."

"But…Lydia." Her gaze searched his face.

"We aren't where you and Drew are. Not by a long shot." He straightened and grinned. "Besides, I don't plan on getting myself killed. I'm too slippery for that."

"Drew will never allow it." No, he'd order Steve to step down and go himself. "We'll all go. We'll be a united front." She grasped at straws, then faced Martin, resigned. "Are you sure this will work?"

"Absolutely." He nodded. "Confront him, threaten him with arrest…you've already taken his son. He'll definitely retaliate."

All her nightmares hit her with the force of tsunami. She started to hyperventilate.

"Head down, darling." Steve pulled her chair out and pushed her head between her knees, waving the guard away. "We're fine, sir. Thank you. Breathe in, then out. That's my girl."

She pushed his hands away. "I'm okay." She took a deep breath in through her nose, then slowly out her mouth before straightening. "Let's bring this man down."

~

Kamal woke in his bed at Devonne's. It had taken one phone call to his uncle to get him released from the jail cell. Now, his uncle had said he'd stay out of sight for a while. Learn the bookkeeping side of the business until things died down.

He couldn't even go to school. As much as his uncle wanted him to, he now said it was too dangerous. Fine by him. He knew his uncle had something to do with his mother's beating. Once he could prove that he had, he'd make sure his uncle never ordered a hit on anyone again.

Without his burner phone which he'd had to turn over at the jail, he couldn't communicate with the detectives. Kamal was truly on his own now.

He sat up and glanced at the room service menu on the nightstand. Choosing a ham and cheese omelet, he ordered breakfast before heading to the shower. Wealth did have certain privileges. Unfortunately, his uncle's wealth had blood on it.

A banging on his door pulled him from the shower. "Your breakfast is here," one of his uncle's goons said. "Devonne said to eat it with him."

Kamal groaned. The more time he spent in his uncle's presence, the harder it was to pretend he'd accepted the lifestyle. "Two minutes."

He dressed as quickly as possible, then hurried to join his uncle at the round table near the window.

"This is how it should be." Devonne smiled. "Father and son having a meal together." His smile didn't meet his eyes.

Blood chilling, appetite gone, Kamal stared at his omelet.

"Seems you were seen talking to a detective yesterday behind your mama's house. The person who saw you said the two of you seemed real friendly. Mind telling me about your conversation?" He picked up his coffee cup and peered over the rim.

Stick as close to the truth as possible. "She wanted to know what I was doing there and whether I was involved in the shooting."

"Why do I feel as if there is more to the story?" He set his cup down with a thunk. "Are you working with them?"

"No. Why would you think that?" His hand shook as he reached for his fork.

"You went from being very reluctant to working with me to being willing."

"You threatened Lincoln. I've come to enjoy…this life." His stomach churned.

"Son, you do realize that if you betray me there is a steep price, don't you?"

"Yes, sir."

"Good." Devonne cut into his steak. "Now we don't have any misunderstandings, do we?"

"No. What about when Martin gets out?"

"I'll handle that."

~

Drew gritted his teeth so hard his jaw ached. He couldn't believe what Linn and Steve were telling him. Use one of his people as bait? No way.

When they'd finished, he stood and shrugged into his jacket. "I'll be the one speaking to Devonne." His gaze landed on Steve, who gave a slow nod. Good. If something happened, the other man would take care of Linn.

"I can do this," Steve said.

"No." Drew shook his head. "I'm the chief. It's my place."

"Don't do this." Linn got to her feet and wrapped her arms around his waist, laying her cheek against his chest. "Please."

Steve left the room, giving them some privacy.

"I have to. Kids are dying. The violence is affecting people not involved in the gangs. A mother of three was killed yesterday. This has to stop." He closed his eyes and breathed deep of her scent, strawberry and vanilla shampoo, a floral perfume. He took another deep breath, imprinting the feel and smell of her on his heart.

He peeled her arms from around him and held her at arm's length. "I need to go." He cupped her face and kissed her. "I'll be home by suppertime."

"You promise?"

He smiled and kissed her again. He couldn't promise. The threat of him being killed was far greater than his returning home alive.

"Don't distract me with kisses." She stepped back. "This is what we discussed last night. This is what we're both so afraid of, and now you're walking headfirst into a bullet." Tears shimmered in her eyes. "I'm sorry I made you sleep on the sofa last night."

He laughed. "I shouldn't have broached my concerns in quite that way. Walk me out?"

"Yes." She slipped her hand in his and walked with him to his car.

As he backed away, he kept his gaze locked on hers for as long as possible. When he had to turn away, he prayed that wouldn't be the last time he saw her.

~

"What's going on?" Lydia turned to Steve, concern on her face. "Something bad is happening, isn't it?"

"He's going to try and get Devonne to kill him."

"What?" Her eyes widened.

"Martin says it's the only way to get Devonne on something he can't buy his way out of. I tried to get him to send me."

"Why?" She took his hand. "Why would you do that?"

"He's going to marry Linn soon. I've nothing holding me here."

"Nothing?" She caressed his cheek. "I'm here. Am I nothing?"

His gaze roamed the roundness of her cheek, the fullness of her lips, the dark eyes framed with long lashes. "We're—"

"You called me sweetheart when I lay on the sidewalk. Did you mean it or do you call all the girls by that endearment?"

"You were conscious?"

"Answer the question."

"I meant it." He leaned his forehead against hers. "Despite the fact you drive you crazy, I'm growing to care for you."

"Good. I'm glad you're here." She glanced to where Linn shuffled to her office. "But, my heart aches for her."

So did his. "Excuse me. I need to go to her. She shouldn't be alone. Will you be alright?"

"I'll make coffee and order in sandwiches. Go. I'm just fine."

With a nod, he rushed to the office the three of them shared and closed the door behind him. "Linn."

She turned and laid her head on his shoulder.

His arms wrapped around her.

"Tell me he's going to be okay even if you have to lie."

"Drew will be just fine." He prayed he wasn't lying. He had a chance at a real relationship, but knew he'd stick by Linn if something happened to Drew. Giving up a life with Lydia, a possible life with a wife and family, wouldn't be possible. He'd never leave his best friend alone.

"Waiting for him to walk back through those doors will be the hardest, longest, thing I've ever had to do." Linn heaved a sigh and sank into her desk chair.

"Lydia is ordering sandwiches." His shoulders slumped. Stupid thing to say.

A sad smile graced her lips. "That's nice." She pulled her cell phone from her pocket. "I can at least know where he is at all times. We've both got a tracking app."

Knowing she'd be glued to the tiny screen, he sat at his desk and booted up his computer. It really was going to be a long day. He glanced up with relief a while later when Lydia entered with coffee and sub sandwiches.

"Hope you're hungry." She passed out their lunch, sending several worried glances Linn's way.

"Stop looking at me like that. I'm fine. I'm doing my best to remain professional and distant. You're constantly reminding me that inwardly I'm terrified. Thanks for the food." Linn returned her attention to her phone.

"He at Devonne's?" Steve asked.

"For the last ten minutes. How long do you think he'll be there?"

"Half hour?" He shrugged. "Depends on how talkative Devonne is."

"I'm not sure y'all want to hear this, but…" Lydia unwrapped her sandwich. "Devonne posted bail for Kamal last night. He's presumed to be with his uncle."

"That's not good." The boy wouldn't last a week on the street.

# Chapter Eighteen

Drew had been surprised to see Kamal standing at his uncle's right. The boy looked as if he'd bolt if someone whispered "Boo". Then, the conversation, if it could be called one, with Devonne had been cut down before Drew could get two words out.

"I see the chief-of-police showing up here as a show of force." Devonne's eyes hardened. "First, my son is arrested without evidence, now you show up. Why?"

"Kamal is a person of interest in yesterday's shooting." Drew squared his shoulders. "You are a suspect in the beating of Tanisha Williams."

He gave a one-shouldered shrug. "What motive would I have?"

"If not you, then who?"

"Someone with a grudge." He steepled his fingers. "You must know we're in a war, correct?"

Drew nodded.

"And that there are casualties? Collateral damage, I

believe it's called."

"Unfortunately. I'm here to take you in for questioning, Mr. Williams. We can do this the easy way or the hard way." He reached for the cuffs hanging on his belt.

Devonne made a motion with his hand.

Something hard struck Drew across the shoulders, knocking him to his knees.

"I guess it'll be the hard way, Chief. Take him to a field somewhere and teach him a lesson."

"Too afraid to do your dirty work here?" Drew bit back a groan. "Why not do it yourself?"

Devonne laughed. "You know that isn't how it's done. Don't worry. You'll only wish you were dead when they finish with you. Make it look like the Indigos did this."

Two of the man's thugs grabbed him by the shoulders. Drew yanked free, getting to his feet. If they were going to take him, he'd get some punches in first.

"No." Kamal rushed forward only to be held back by another of his uncle's men.

"Don't get in this, son." Drew threw a punch catching one man in the chin. He whirled to get another in the stomach, before a Tazer had him flopping on the floor as fire burned through his side.

Two men slung his arms over their shoulders and dragged him from the room. He struggled when they reached the elevator only to be hit over the head. Blackness engulfed him.

He woke in the trunk of a car with no room to move. His bulk could barely be squeezed in. His arms tingled from loss of circulation.

Gravel crunched under the tires. Okay, a dirt road.

There were hundreds of dirt roads in the state. Had they taken his phone?

He tried with no success to reach for his pocket. If they'd taken it, Linn would have no way of locating him. He could very well die today. With the gangs committing crimes and trying to pin the deeds on each other, he didn't have much hope for a good outcome.

The vehicle stopped. A few seconds later, the trunk opened. Hands grabbed him and rolled him to the ground, before hefting him to his feet. Someone cut the zip ties binding his wrists. Without waiting for feeling to return to Drew's hands and feet, someone thrust a fist into his stomach.

His breath left him a whoosh. He barely had time to straighten before four men circled him and started hitting and kicking. Definitely not a fair fight.

A fist connected with his eye. The skin split, and blood trickled down his face. A kick to the back of his leg knocked him to the ground. Drew couldn't manage a single punch, the hits and kicks came so fast.

He curled into the fetal position and folded his hands over his head in a vain attempt to protect himself.

One of the men tossed his cell phone on the ground in front of him and dropped a rock on the device, shattering it and rendering it useless.

Drew tried getting to his feet. He wouldn't die without a fight. Something hard struck him across the back, and he fell. A few more whacks with what he could now see was a stick as thick as his forearm, and he lost consciousness. His last coherent thought was to tell Linn he was sorry about leaving her.

~

"How could you take the chief?" Kamal paced the floor, no longer caring whether Devonne saw the worry on his face. "Do you know the trouble that will bring?"

"Not if the authorities think the Indigos did it. Why do you care?" His uncle narrowed his eyes. "Why do you think I did this?"

He stopped and met the cold stare of Devonne. "To teach me a lesson."

"Smart boy." He grinned. "I figured you were leaking information to the cops. Mind telling me why? I am your father."

"You're not. Martin is my father." Kamal's hands curled into fists. "I don't want this life."

"You have a problem with money?"

"No, I have a problem with killing. I'd rather live in a box in Homeless Park, then follow in your footsteps." Please let the chief be alive. He would be able to tell the others that this was Devonne's orders. No one would believe Kamal, the son of a gang lord.

"Go to your room while I figure out what to do with a traitor of a son." He snapped his fingers for one of his goons to escort Kamal.

Once inside, he heard the audible click of the door being locked from the other side. He plopped onto the bed. So much for his plan of getting out of jail. He was no match for his uncle's sharp mind. All he'd done is make things worse.

He fell backward trying to think of a way out of the crater he'd dug. How could he make it up to the detective if the chief died because of him. He really wanted Martin out of jail, collect Lincoln and his mom, and go somewhere no one would ever find them.

~

"Drew's last location was here." Linn shoved her phone under Steve's nose. "That's nowhere near Devonne's, and he hasn't moved."

A big man in a leather jacket turned from the receptionist desk. "The chief is missing? I can rally the boys and go looking for him."

"I think I know where he is, but thank you." She knew the man belonged to the large group of bikers that patrolled town.

"We could start at that gang's place, then follow the trail to his last location. Might pick up some clues that way."

"Okay." Her and Steve would go directly to the location she'd last seen Drew's blinking blue dot.

The biker darted out the door. Soon the roar of engines filled the air as they sped from the parking lot.

"What did he want?" Steve asked.

Lucy shrugged. "He never had the chance to say. I hope you find the chief."

They would. The alternative couldn't happen. Linn raced from the building, Steve right next to her, leaving Lydia to hold down the fort.

"I'm driving this time." Steve snatched the keys from her hand. "You keep your eye on the coordinates and give me directions."

No argument from her. The way her hands trembled, she'd be a danger behind the wheel.

Steve sped down the highway, turning when she said only slowing when she said there had to be a turnoff somewhere to their right. "Over the railroad tracks. There."

She pointed to a barricade that had been moved to the side. The grass looked freshly driven over.

Steve whipped in that direction, sending them hurtling over the tracks and onto a dirt road. "How much farther?"

"Maybe a football field. It isn't exact." She leaned forward and stared out the window. "What is that in the road?"

Something that looked like a big black bag of garbage lay in the middle of the road. "Stop or you'll run over it."

Dust flew as he skidded to a halt a few feet in front of the bag.

Heart in a throat as dry as the road they drove on, Linn exited the car and approached the bag. A groan. Slight movement. "Steve!"

She ripped at the opening of the bag revealing hair the color of wheat. "It's Drew." Beaten almost beyond recognition and thrown away like trash. "Oh, baby." She gathered him in her arms. "Call an ambulance."

The roar of motorcycles approached. The bikers surrounded them.

"Who did this?" The leader asked. "Who would do this to our chief?"

"I don't..."

"Devonne." Drew coughed and opened one eye into a slit. "Wants it to look like the Indigos did it. We have to get out of here. Those men didn't go far."

Linn glanced around the area. An indigo strip of fabric fluttered from a barbed wire fence. "How do you know they didn't leave?"

"They said they were laying a trap to get rid of several pigs at a time."

Her blood chilled.

Steve propped his shoulder under Drew's arm. "Let's get out of here."

Between the two of them, they were able to get Drew laid out on the backseat. He couldn't stretch, but at least he was off the ground.

"Let's get you to a hospital."

"We'll stay right by you." One of the bikers said. The others nodded.

Their presence gave Linn some comfort. She'd fall apart over Drew's condition later. Right now, she had a job to do.

"What happened, Drew?" She asked as Steve made a U-turn in the road.

"Our plan almost didn't work." He gasped and struggled to a sitting position. "I went in to arrest Devonne. Kamal was there."

"Yeah, we heard his uncle paid the bail."

"Anyway, it didn't take long for them to start hitting. All part of Devonne's plan to get rid of us and walk away free at the same time. Only one fault in that plan." The corner of his mouth quirked. "I didn't die."

Thank God. She reached over the seat and took his hand. "Is there anywhere on you that doesn't—whoa." She slammed into the door as Steve jerked the wheel.

"We've got company."

She peered over to see several vehicles speeding from a side road.

The motorcycles formed a tighter circle around Linn's jeep.

Steve increased their speed. "This is going to be bad."

"Just get us out of here." Linn pulled her weapon.

A shot rang out.

One of the bikers fell, his bike skidding along the interstate into the ditch, taking the rider with him.

Linn fired into the window of the closest car. "I can't hold them off on my own."

"Give me a gun," Drew said. "I can see a bit."

"Linn, give him mine. I need two hands on the wheel." Steve glanced over.

She pulled his service revolver from his shoulder holster and handed it to Drew. "Be careful."

A semi-truck swerved to avoid the shooting cars and overturned on the median. Cars slammed on their brakes or cut across the median to head in the opposite direction.

Linn didn't blame them. Sticking around with bullets flying would get them killed. She shrieked as the back windshield shattered.

"I'm okay." Drew returned fire.

Another biker fell, this one hitting a tree on the side of the road.

Linn swallowed against the tears in her throat at the loss of their guardians. Her next shot took out the tire of the nearest car, sending it crashing.

They lost three bikers by the time they disabled the two cars chasing them. "Stay in the car," Linn ordered. "You aren't in charge right now."

"The hell I ain't." Drew winced as he reached for the doorknob.

"Call for help." Shaking her head, weapon at the ready, Linn approached one of the vehicles while Steve checked the other.

Injured, but not dead, three young men wearing green glared from each car.

"Toss your guns out or I'll shoot you right here and deal with the repercussions later." She waved her weapon.

One by one, guns and automatic rifles were tossed out the windows.

"What I ought to do is let the surviving bikers have a go at you. I doubt they feel too kindly after you killed a few of their friends." She'd like nothing more than to look the other way for a few minutes. "But, I take my job seriously. Out of the car and kneel on the shoulder, hands folded behind your heads."

Soon, all six knelt in the grass at the edge of the interstate. A chopper whirled overhead.

Great. The local news had already gotten wind of the shootout.

Drew, arm tight against his waist, approached at a slow pace. He stood and glared down at the teens who stared back with defiance. He made a noise in his throat. "I'm going to make sure you spend a very long time in prison along with the man you've pledged loyalty to. But, considering you seriously messed up by leaving me alive, I doubt you'll live that long."

Linn agreed. Devonne wasn't one to let such a serious thing alone.

# Chapter Nineteen

Kamal picked the lock and opened his door after midnight, moving as slow as possible. The hotel they stayed in kept everything in such good shape that his door didn't make a sound. The burner phone he'd hidden behind the dresser seemed to weigh a ton in his pocket. If he were caught, Devonne would know for sure that Kamal was a snitch.

After peeking into the living room of the suite, he tiptoed past the snoozing guard and into the kitchen. Devonne would have a fit about the man sleeping on the job, but Kamal couldn't stay imprisoned another night. He had to get out and contact the detective about the chief.

He unlocked the deadbolt, freezing at the click. When the guard didn't come, he opened the door and stepped out. He closed the door behind him, then made a mad dash for the elevator. Getting past the front desk would be his biggest challenge.

The elevator seemed to move in slow motion. Kamal held his breath as the doors open, relaxing a bit when no one waited to get on. He stepped into the hall and looked both ways. When no one came for him, he sprinted for the delivery door at the back.

A siren wailed as he slammed it open. Not stopping to see who would come for him, he increased his speed, wanting to put as much distance between him and the hotel as possible. He could hide in a lot of places on foot.

Shouts echoed down the alley. Kamal turned left and climbed a fence. On a new street, he continued his run for freedom, going down one street then another until he could no longer hear sounds of pursuit. Then, he hunkered behind a bush in someone's yard and called Detective MacFarland.

"Kamal?" She asked, her voice hoarse with sleep.

"Is the chief okay?"

"He's in the hospital, but he'll be fine in a few days. How are you?"

"I'm sorry." He started to cry. "I couldn't stop them from taking him."

"I know, sweetie. Where are you?"

"I got away."

"Okay." She sounded awake now. "I want you to memorize this address and get there however you can. You must be careful not to be followed. Don't lead trouble to Lincoln. Mrs. Richards will take good care of you. Call me when you get there. I'll come for you, but I'm pretty sure I have eyes on me." She rattled off an address. "Do you have money?"

"Yes. I'll catch the bus as far as I can." He hung up and pocketed the phone before heading to the nearest bus stop. The last one would run at one thirty. He stopped. The bus stop was lit up like a neon sign.

Devonne would think to look there first. Kamal glanced around the area. He couldn't ask his old boss for help. It needed to be a stranger, but who would give a strange black teenager a ride at that time of the night?

He approached a pizza delivery guy. "I'll give you two hundred dollars to drive me somewhere."

"Sure. I just finished my shift. How far is it?"

"I don't know." He gave the guy the address, and he punched it into a GPS. "An hour drive for two hundred bucks? You got it. Get in."

Kamal paid him and dove into the backseat and slouched. "Thanks."

"No problem. You're paying me." The man laughed and pulled away from the curve.

Kamal kept up a constant surveillance as they traveled, glancing behind them on a regular basis. The chances of them being followed were slim. Who would suspect a pizza guy? Still, he wasn't taking any chances.

"Dude, we're here. Doesn't look like anyone is awake. Are they expecting you?"

Kamal opened his eyes. "Not exactly, but it's fine. Thanks." He shoved open his door and stared at the house.

Pure country. Like something you'd see on one of them Hallmark channels. He took a deep breath and marched toward the porch as the pizza guy drove away.

"Stop right there." An old woman armed with a rifle stepped onto the porch. "It's not usually a good thing when someone arrives before three a.m."

"It's Kamal Williams. You have my brother."

"You alone?"

"Yes, ma'am. Detective MacFarland sent me."

She lowered her weapon. "Then come on in, son." She held the door open. "Your brother has been missing you."

"Where is he?" He stepped into the house full of more things than his mother had ever owned.

"Upstairs, last door on the right. There's another bed in there. You hungry?"

"No, ma'am." He climbed the stairs, stared at his little brother's sleeping face, and started to cry. Lincoln was just fine. Kamal would be fine. All they had to do now was get their mother to safety.

~

Linn opened her eyes to see Drew staring at a food tray on the hospital bed table. "What's wrong?"

"Soft foods?" He glanced at her, the one eye he could open a little wider than the day before. "My stomach isn't hurt."

"Maybe it's protocol. You're beat up pretty bad, a few cracked ribs. A fractured jaw. Be grateful you aren't eating through a straw." She touched his hand, the only thing not bruised that she could see. "You can't open your mouth all the way, sweetheart. I'm sure that's the reason for the soft food."

He sighed and took a bite of lime Jell-O.

"Kamal called last night. He managed to escape his uncle. I sent him to Mrs. Richards."

"He call you once he got there?"

She shook her head. "Not yet, and he isn't answering his phone. I'm going to call Mrs. Richards."

"Good idea."

A nurse entered the room to take Drew's vitals, so Linn stepped out of the room to make her call. After a few rings,

Mrs. Richards answered.

"Did Kamal make it safely?"

"He just woke up. Poor thing took one look at his brother and cried, then went to bed. I'm going to feed him pancakes. He'll be right as rain in an hour or two. Do you need to speak to him?"

"No, just wanted to make sure he made it there. Thanks." She hung up and sat back in the chair in Drew's room. He drank beef broth from a bowl with a straw.

"The doctor said the chief will be here for a few days," the nurse said. "Those ribs need to heal a bit before he starts moving around."

Linn grinned. They'd already figured out it would be hard to keep him down. When the nurse left, she asked, "How do we get you a guard outside the door? Once Devonne realizes you're alive, he'll send someone for you."

As much as she wanted to, she couldn't stay with him around the clock. She still had a job that needed doing. They couldn't stop the gangs by sitting around.

"The FBI should arrive today. I called Lucy and told her to send them to me when they do. Little Rock's SWAT team is also arriving." His gaze pierced Linn's. "You'll need to take the lead on this since I'm down."

"I can do this." She squared her shoulders. "Steve and I will take the lead together. He's more logical."

Drew laughed, then winced. "Yes, he is. The two of you make a good team." He sighed. "I sure wish I could finish this with you."

"Me, too." She leaned over and placed a tender kiss on his lips. "I'll keep you posted. Now, about that guard."

He motioned toward the drawer in the bed table. "Got

my gun. I'll sleep with it within an arm's reach. I'll be fine. The hospital security guard will check on me."

"I love you."

"I love you, too. Don't get yourself killed, okay? I couldn't live through it."

Another kiss, and she left, headed for the office.

Steve glanced up from his desk when she entered. "Drew okay?"

"He will be. FBI and SWAT are due sometime today. Then, Drew wants to talk to them. He's put us in charge."

"The end is in sight."

"Hopefully." She sat at her desk. "Headache gone, Lydia?"

"Absolutely." The rookie grinned.

"Good. We're going to need you."

~

Steve still hadn't gotten used to the fact that Lydia cared for him. They hadn't known each other long, but rather than look at her as a little sister, which he'd thought to do, he'd grown to…dare he say love her? Or maybe begin to love her?

His gaze followed as she left the room.

"Smitten, are you?" Linn grinned, propping her feet on her desk.

"Maybe." He stood as three men and two women in dark suits stood in the doorway.

"Chief Wayne?"

"He's in the hospital." Linn got up and extended her hand. "I'm Detective MacFarland, this is Detective Chavez. We're in charge at this point, although the chief has requested you pay him a visit in the hospital so he can fill you in. SWAT team?"

"At the motel on 40 waiting instructions. I'm Agent Larson, these are Wells, Shields, Black, and Swanson." The bald man handed her a card. "We're also at the motel. Here's my number. I'd like to convene in the conference room in two hours to formulate a plan of attack." He gave her a stern nod, then marched away, the others following.

"It doesn't look as if we're in charge." Steve arched a brow. "We've been delegated to a minion, I think."

"As long as we stop this gang war, I don't care if Goofy is in charge." She fell back into her chair. "Hopefully, they'll work with us rather than push us to the side."

Steve didn't care who the top gun was as long as the job got done. He wanted the crime and the killing to stop. For Upton Falls to return to the town it was before The Photographer showed up. Had it really only been a little over a year?

Linn and he hadn't been partners for long when the killings started. Women like her dying in a scarlet dress with a red rose next to them. His twin had been trying to find a substitute for his obsession. Linn had almost died then. The fact she hadn't had been the beginning of Steve's respect for the cowboy FBI agent, now Chief Wayne. There was no other man he would've stepped back and let have Linn's heart without a fight.

Now, Drew lay in the hospital, and it was up to Steve to keep Linn safe. The daunting task sent ripples of dread up his spine. He'd do everything in his power to keep his promise.

Lydia joined them, chattering about the rude FBI agents. He'd have to keep her safe, too.

Even if it meant his life.

# Chapter Twenty

Kamal opened his eyes to the grinning face of Lincoln leaning over him. "Hey, little man."

"You came, just like you said you would." His brother wrapped his arms around his neck.

"You bet." Kamal sat. "I'm not going to leave you again." He prayed he could keep that promise.

"Where's momma?"

"I'm not sure, but we'll find her. Dad gets out of jail soon. We'll be a family again." He took Lincoln's hand and led him to the kitchen where Mrs. Richards made breakfast.

"Good morning. Lincoln said I had to make biscuits and chocolate gravy for him. Do you prefer peanut butter or butter?" She grinned.

"I don't think I've ever had chocolate gravy," he said.

"Then one of each. Sit, there's orange juice."

If not for the Glock sitting on the kitchen counter, Kamal would've thought he was in any TV grandma's kitchen. He poured two glasses of orange juice from a heavy pitcher and handed one to his brother.

"What do y'all do all day?"

"Schoolwork, then game shows." She laughed. "I've got your brother loving them."

"You've been schooling him?" Kamal grinned for the first time in a long time.

"Of course. He can't fall behind. Besides, he's a smart boy. You'll be getting online school too while you're here."

A sudden urge to stay in the so very old white woman country house washed over him. At closer look, every surface at a knickknack or a blanket of some kind. It was almost as if the house had wrapped its arms around him and called him home.

"Kamal, take your brother to the closet under the stairs. He knows the way." Mrs. Richards's hand inched toward the gun. "Go on, now. It's probably nothing, but call the detective, please."

He glanced out the window to see a wine-colored Cadillac cruise past the house. A car that definitely looked out of place on that country road. "I can help."

"Do as I say." Gone was the cheerful Grandma. She'd morphed into an army sergeant.

Kamal grabbed Lincoln and headed for the stairs. His little brother did a strange tapping sequence on a wood panel, and a section of the wall slid open. Wow. He ducked and stepped into a tiny room full of books, toys, pillows and blankets. A small fridge had been shoved in one corner. Shelves held food. Very cramped, but able to sustain a person or two for a week.

"Have you been in here before?" Kamal left the panel open a crack. He needed to be able to hear in case Mrs.

Richards needed him.

"No, but we've practiced." Lincoln sat cross-legged. "I always get a cookie after practice."

Kamal peered through the opening he'd left. He could catch a glimpse of one of Mrs. Richards shoulders as she kept her back pressed to the wall.

He pulled out his phone and called the detective.

"How are you liking there?" she asked.

"Mrs. Richards has a gun, and she's acting all Rambo. Some pimped out car is going up and down the road. She told me to call you."

"Stay safe. I'll be there in an hour or less. Keep me updated." Click.

Kamal pressed his eye to the opening again. As much as he wanted to help the old woman, he'd slam the hiding place closed in a heartbeat for Lincoln's safety.

~

Steve caught Lydia's gaze from across the conference table and winked. They'd stayed up late the night before enjoying a dinner and a glass of wine. Talked about everything and nothing. Snuggled, got a little heated, then pulled back, testing the boundaries of their foundling relationship.

Pink dusted her cheeks. She ducked her head, but not before he saw the smile.

They'd been in the conference room for two hours going over the same details over and over like a stuck record. What were they waiting for?

He'd heard the grumblings of the SWAT team that morning before heading to the station. They'd expected to act immediately.

Something nudged his foot. Lydia glanced up from lowered lashes.

Linn elbowed him. "Larson is watching," she hissed.

Steve grinned behind his hand. "I don't care."

"You're acting like a teenager."

"Something to say, Detective?" Larson arched a brow.

"Only that we should be out there taking down some gangs." She met his gaze with a sharp one.

Steve recognized the signs of Linn reaching her end. The poor agent had no idea what was coming. Linn could knock him down a peg or two, and Steve wanted to see it.

He pulled his leg back so his foot couldn't touch Lydia's and did his best not to look too bored as Larson droned on.

The ringing of Linn's phone broke through and everyone turned to stare.

"Sorry. Have to take this." She mouthed "Devonne."

~

"Another suspicious vehicle driving by Mrs. Richards. I'm headed out." Lydia slipped her phone into her purse.

"Now?" Agent Larson frowned.

"Yes, sir. You'll have to carry on without me." Not that it would be difficult for them. Larson acted as if any opinion from a woman could be discarded outright. She glanced at Steve who started to get to his feet.

"No, Detective MacFarland can go herself," the agent said. "We need the manpower."

"Excuse me." Linn frowned. "I'm the one left in charge here. If I say Detective Chavez comes with me, then he does. I'm sure the four of you can keep going over the details until the town erupts in a war. As for me and Steve, we're going to the aid of a couple of children."

Head high, she marched from the room, knowing Steve would be right there with her.

"That was fun to watch." Steve jogged alongside her. "I don't think the agent is used to being shot down by a woman."

She laughed. "It felt good. Now, let's go run off another carful of gangster kids."

"You don't think there's cause for concern?" He slid into the passenger seat.

"There's always reason. I'll break the speed record getting there, but I really do hope it's just more of the teens trying to be tough rather than a real confrontation." She glanced at her phone. "No more communication." Which she hoped meant Kamal saw no new reason to call.

"How's Drew?"

"Bruised from head-to-toe, but they released him home last night." She turned onto the Interstate. "He'll be bored out of his mind, but doctor's orders that he stay home for at least three days."

The closer they got to Mrs. Richards, the more serious she got. The more time that passed without Kamal getting in touch again started to worry her. She didn't think the car would drive back and forth this long. The fact that no one had called her to say the danger was past, filled her veins with ice water. What if they hadn't got in touch because they couldn't?

Steve must have checked his ammunition ten times. "I think we need to call Larson for backup."

"Me, too. My senses have been tingling the last fifteen minutes."

Steve made the call. "They're coming. They'll be half an hour behind us."

"I'm not slowing down."

"Not asking you to."

She pressed the accelerator, then slowed to take the proper exit. The sharp turn had them heading uncomfortably close to the barricade, but she managed to keep the jeep on the road.

When they turned onto the road to Mrs. Richards's house, a burgundy Cadillac blocked the way.

One man, wearing a dark shirt and carrying an automatic rifle, approached the jeep. "There's a war about to start in town. Devonne wants his son there to see him win."

"I'm not letting you take him." Linn met the man's cold stare with one of her own.

He raised the gun. "He figured you'd say that, so told me to bring you a long as collateral. This is what is going to happen, ma'am. You're going to get out of the car. Your partner is not. You'll then go with me to get the kid. After that, we're in this car. If you don't comply, I'll shoot your partner and my man whacks the old woman and kid. Either way, Devonne's son is coming with me."

"Okay." Keeping her hands up as much as possible, she got out of the car.

"Do not shoot me," he told Steve. "A man I have watching will then kill Detective MacFarland."

Linn gave Steve a nod. She didn't really believe that Devonne would kill her once he had Kamal. He'd think he'd made his point with Drew. Still, she couldn't shrug off the niggle of fear at the base of her neck as she headed for the house, her captor so close behind her she could smell the cologne he wore. Something sweet.

Mrs. Richards and the two boys sat on the steps of the house while an armed man rocked on the porch.

"This is far enough. Come on, boy."

Kamal glanced from the man to Linn. At her nod, he came to them.

"Now, let the others go." Linn glanced over her shoulder.

He waved the other man forward. "Let's go. We're on a tight schedule." He marched them to the car, shoved them in, and then had them speeding back down the mountain at a rate that sent her stomach into her throat. They rocketed past a black Suburban which looked suspiciously like the one Larson rode.

They sped through Upton Falls where groups of young men in different colored shirts were facing off. No sign of the feds, although the SWAT team van sat at one end of Main Street in front of the police station. No pedestrians strolled the sidewalk. Shades were being drawn on shops closing up for safety. War had come to Upton Falls.

Linn reached over and took Kamal's hand. "It'll be alright. Everyone is safe." Devonne wouldn't kill his son. Not if he truly believed he'd have a dynasty to leave his heir.

The car stopped near the lake's marina. Linn and Kamal were marched between several armed men to a waiting yacht. Crime must pay very well.

Two men accompanied them onto the boat. One man stood at the wheel. Seconds later, the boat skimmed across the water.

Linn sat on a cushioned bench at the back and pulled Kamal down with her. She put her arm around him as if to comfort him and whispered, "It'll only take about twenty minutes to get to the other marina. We're going to have to jump and swim. Tell me you can swim."

"I can." He trembled. "Just not very good."

"All you have to do is swim good enough. When I say jump, you jump and dive. You'll have to go underwater as far as possible, understand? We'll jump to our left and swim straight toward the bank."

He nodded. "Then what?"

"We get to the station."

The boat's captain focused on the water. The two, armed goons smoked cigarettes next to him. None of them paid her and Kamal any attention.

"Ready?" She glanced at Kamal.

"Yes."

"Jump."

They leaped from the bench into the murky water of the lake. Linn dove, knowing the dark water would shield her for as long as she could hold her breath. Come on, Kamal, you can do this.

When her lungs needed air, she rose slowly to the surface and glanced around for the boy. There. Almost to the bank. Good boy.

The men on the yacht shouted and pointed. The yacht started to turn.

She dove again and swam after Kamal. She surfaced again to see the yacht struggling to turn around in the alcove the two of them had swam into. Good. Unless they were willing to get wet, she didn't see anyone jumping off the boat. Most likely, they'd call someone on land to give chase.

On the bank, she met up with Kamal who leaned against

a tree and tried to catch his breath. "You okay?"

He nodded. "That was a lot of swimming."

She chuckled. "You did great. Stay close. We have to get through without any of the gang members seeing us." A gigantic task when you had each part of the street leading to the station lined with a SWAT team and three rival gangs. All who knew who Kamal's father was.

They ducked down alleys and behind dumpsters, even scaling a fence or two to come around back of the station. She glanced both ways across the parking lot of the strip mall behind the station. Free and clear.

"Run to that gray door. I'm right behind you." She pointed.

He took off like an Olympic runner. Linn didn't waste any time either. They banged through the back door, Linn locking it behind her, and into the bull pen just as Steve charged through the front door.

His eyes widened at the sight of her. "Why are you all wet?"

"We jumped off Devonne's boat. This was the safest place I could think of to bring Kamal during a gang war." None of them would be completely safe until it was over.

# Chapter Twenty-One

Kamal sat wrapped in a blanket, while Linn nursed a cup of coffee. So far, they'd been back over half an hour with no shots being fired. She peered out the window. The rivals still faced off against each other, although their body language and hurled insults were escalating.

"The waiting makes you almost wish they'd start shooting." Steve stepped up beside her. "Can I ask you something?"

"Absolutely."

"Don't you think it strange that the agents never seemed in a hurry to try rounding up the gang leaders?" He faced her.

"Yep." She met his gaze. "I think Larson isn't being forthright with us. The other agents are all new to field work. They'd follow his lead without question. Yes, I'm very suspicious." Having seen how Drew operated when he was FBI, Larson was the opposite.

Speaking of the devil, the four agents pulled into the parking lot. Without glancing toward the upcoming battle,

Larson led the others inside. His gaze went straight to Kamal. "Glad to see he's safe."

Linn simply nodded and turned her attention back to outside. "Now that everyone is here, lock the doors."

"They'll burn us out," Larson said.

"Lock the doors." She didn't look his way. Locking the doors would make it harder for someone to get to Kamal. She wasn't worried about a fire on a brick building. Not yet, anyway.

Drew's car pulled into the parking lot. "Hold up." She exhaled heavily. "You told him about my abduction, didn't you, Steve?"

"I made the man a promise to keep him up-to-date. Your fiancé has a right to know." He emphasized fiancé.

Drew climbed slowly from his vehicle and made his way just as slow to the building. Catching sight of Linn through the glass door, he smiled and moved a bit faster. "You're here."

"Went swimming." She cupped his cheek. "You fool. You're supposed to be in bed."

"I'll pull up a chair. There's no way I could stay home with you in the hands of Devonne." He lowered his head, his lips by her ear. "Meet me in my office in five minutes."

"Okay. I'll get you some coffee." She tossed a questioning look at Steve and headed for the breakroom.

Lydia sat at a table and stared into an almost empty cup. "I should never have come here."

"What are you talking about?" Linn reached for the pot.

"This is all because of my grandfather."

"Not all of it." But, the feud between her grandfather and Devonne did play a huge part. "Chin up. We're going to need every hand on deck before this is over." She poured Drew a cup of coffee, topped hers off, and joined him in his office, pleased to see him sitting.

She set the cup in front of him. "How are you feeling?"

"Sore as hell, but grateful. Pain means I'm alive." He motioned for her to close the door. "I won't keep you long. Steve told me of his suspicions regarding Larson, so I've been asking some questions of my FBI friends. Seems he's being watched very closely. An anonymous caller, someone they couldn't prove had merit, reported Larson as being an informant to Devonne."

"Which explains his slow moving in doing anything."

"Exactly. Now, we have to prove him dirty."

"That won't be—" The sounds of a gunfight sounded outside. She bolted to her feet. "We'll talk later." She rushed from the room. "Give the order for the SWAT team to take action. Smoke bombs and rubber bullets only. We don't need a street full of dead kids." She glanced at Larson. "Now."

Frowning, he spoke into his radio and gave the order.

Lydia entered the room and stood by Steve. He put an arm around her waist and pulled her close.

Linn smiled, happy for her friend. Her joy quickly faded at the scene of violence raging outside.

A black Cadillac drove slowly toward the fight, stopping a few yards away. Devonne got out, a rifle slung over his shoulder as he marched toward the scene.

Martin stepped from the shadows and called out his name.

Kamal bolted from his seat.

Devonne turned.

Martin raised a gun and fired. Once, twice, three times,

each bullet making the other man jerk. When Devonne fell and didn't move again, Martin glanced toward the police station. Meeting Linn's shocked gaze, he nodded, then darted away.

"Are we going after him?" Lydia asked. "He's a felon with a gun and just committed murder."

Linn's gaze locked with Kamal's. "We'll have to when this is over. You realize that, right? We will have to do what we can to locate him and arrest him."

"I know." The boy squared his shoulders. "He did this to keep my family safe."

That's why the last thing Linn wanted was to put the man behind bars again.

The fighting outside died down. Linn unlocked the doors. "Time to get to work. Kamal, you stay here with Drew. Make sure he doesn't try to follow us."

His eyes widened. "How am I supposed to stop him?"

"Do your best." She clapped him on the shoulder, then marched outside. The SWAT team had the surviving fighters lined up under guard. Ambulances arrived on scene to check on the dead and wounded. A huge price to pay for peace.

Out of the corner of her eye, she spotted Larson marching away. She followed, her gun in her hand. "Where are you going, Agent? Now that Devonne is dead, you have no boss."

He whirled. "What are you talking about?"

"You being on Devonne's payroll. I'm right, aren't I?" She tilted her head. "That's why you took so long to do anything pertaining to this upcoming war. What were you going to get out of letting this war happen? Money?"

"You don't know what you're talking about." His hand

inched toward his weapon.

"I wouldn't, if I were you." Steve stepped around the corner of the drugstore. "We've got enough evidence to bring you in for questioning. Using just your fingertips, lift the gun from its holster and hand it to me. Then, nice and slow, put your hands behind your back."

"Or what? You going to shoot me?"

"I might. Because of you, a lot of young men are dead."

"Gangsters." Larson spit.

"Kids." Linn gritted her teeth and raised her weapon. "Look, Agent. We have a lot of work to do. Either you let me take you in or I shoot you. I don't have time to argue. Now do as Detective Chavez said."

Larson cursed and handed over his weapon. "You have no proof."

"Then you have nothing to worry about. I'll take him in Steve, if you'll take over out here."

"Will do. Lydia will help." Once Larson's hands were cuffed, Steve headed toward the SWAT team.

Linn took the agent to the station and turned him over to Drew. It was over. The worst gang war to ever occur in the state of Arkansas had come to an end.

Her gaze fell on Drew. They were both alive. She smiled.

He returned her smile and led Larson to a holding cell.

~

Three days later, Kamal, Lincoln, and their mother disappeared. Neighbors spotted them getting on a bus, suitcases in hand. It didn't take a genius to figure out they most likely went to meet Martin.

Linn hoped they found a future together. One where the

boys were safe.

She sat on the sofa with Drew's head in her lap. The bruises on his face had faded to a dirty yellow. He moved a little easier now. "I don't want a wedding."

"Why?" He glanced up.

"Let's elope. I want to get married as soon as possible. Start a family."

He sat up, his gaze searching her face. "You sure?"

"Positive. I do want the honeymoon though. We've earned some time away."

He got to his feet and held out his hand. "Then let's go. It'll take two days to get to Vegas. Then, we'll fly out of there to Maui."

She laughed. "You've got it all figured out."

"Been thinking on it for days."

She slipped her hand in his. "Let's pack. I'll send Steve a text letting him know he's on his own for a few days."

"Not really. He seems to be moving forward with Lydia quite nicely." He put his hand on the small of her back and led her to the bedroom.

Her heart did somersaults with each article of clothing that went into the suitcase. They were finally getting married. The last year had been hell except for the love they shared. Now, they'd be partners in name as well as in work.

"I love you." Tears blurred his face.

"I love you, too, sweetheart." He lowered his head and kissed her. One slow, hot, and full of promises.

~

Kamal, or Reece as his new identification stated, slid from his seat on the bus and stepped into the heat of Arizona near the Mexico border. Not too much longer, and his family would be reunited with Martin in Mexico. A new life.

He smiled over at his mother. She moved with a slight limp after her beating, but the cuts and bruises had healed. At least on the outside. The best part was she hadn't had a drink of alcohol or taken drugs in days. The main stipulation in Martin taking her back as his wife.

"Ready?" He asked.

"More than." She lifted her suitcase.

As they crossed the border, Martin greeted them. He wrapped them all in a big hug. "My family. We are together again. No more trouble following us."

Kamal glanced back to the American side, knowing Detective MacFarland wouldn't come after his father in Mexico. Nor would the chief. They were safe.

~

Steve glanced at his phone and laughed. "Linn and Drew are headed to Vegas to get married, then on to Maui."

Lydia glanced up from her desk. "How romantic? Have you ever done anything spur of the moment?"

"They've been planning on getting married for a while now."

"Focus, Steve." She grinned. "We're talking about you now."

"Oh. No, I'm not a very spontaneous guy."

She got up from her desk and perched on the corner of his, toying with his tie. "You could be." Her dark eyes twinkled. "I know we can't take off since there's no one left but us, but one day, maybe…"

Was she saying what he thought she was? "Are you saying we should run off and get married?" His heart leaped. Could he? They hadn't known each other long. Could he take the chance this woman was the one?

"Not today, but yes. Someday." She moved away, tossing over her shoulder. "Surprise me." She blew him a kiss and left the office.

Steve exhaled long and slow, then he smiled. He'd surprise her alright. Once Linn and Drew returned, he'd whisk her away and put a ring on his finger. To make sure he didn't chicken out, he grabbed his jacket. He'd buy the ring that day. With it in his pocket, he'd be thinking every day of making Lydia his wife.

Steps lighter than he could ever remember them being, Steve headed for his car.

The End

www.cynthiahickey.com

Cynthia Hickey is a multi-published and best-selling author of cozy mysteries and romantic suspense. She has taught writing at many conferences and small writing retreats. She and her husband run the publishing press, Winged Publications, which includes some of the CBA's best well-known authors. They live in Arizona and Arkansas, becoming snowbirds with two dogs and one cat. They have ten grandchildren who keep them busy and tell everyone they know that "Nana is a writer."

Connect with me on FaceBook
Twitter
Sign up for my newsletter and receive a free short story
www.cynthiahickey.com

Follow me on Amazon
And Bookbub

Enjoy other books by Cynthia Hickey
**Colors of Evil Series**

Shades of Crimson
Coral Shadows

**Misty Hollow**
Secrets of Misty Hollow
Deceptive Peace

Calm Surface
Lightning Never Strikes Twice
Lethal Inheritance
Bitter Isolation
Say I Don't

**The Tail Waggin' Mysteries**
Cat-Eyed Witness
The Dog Who Found a Body
Troublesome Twosome
Four-Legged Suspect
Unwanted Christmas Guest
Wedding Day Cat Burglar

**Brothers Steele**
Sharp as Steele
Carved in Steele
Forged in Steele
Brothers Steele (All three in one)

**The Brothers of Copper Pass**
Wyatt's Warrant
Dirk's Defense
Stetson's Secret
Houston's Hope
Dallas's Dare
Seth's Sacrifice
Malcolm's Misunderstanding
The Brothers of Copper Pass Boxed Set

**Time Travel**
The Portal

**Tiny House Mysteries**
No Small Caper
Caper Goes Missing
Caper Finds a Clue
Caper's Dark Adventure
A Strange Game for Caper
Caper Steals Christmas
Caper Finds a Treasure
Tiny House Mysteries boxed set

**Wife for Hire – Private Investigators**
Saving Sarah
Lesson for Lacey
Mission for Meghan
Long Way for Lainie
Aimed at Amy
Wife for Hire (all five in one)

**A Hollywood Murder**
Killer Pose, book 1
Killer Snapshot, book 2
Shoot to Kill, book 3
Kodak Kill Shot, book 4
To Snap a Killer
Hollywood Murder Mysteries

**Shady Acres Mysteries**
Beware the Orchids, book 1
Path to Nowhere
Poison Foliage
Poinsettia Madness
Deadly Greenhouse Gases
Vine Entrapment
Shady Acres Boxed Set

## **CLEAN BUT GRITTY Romantic Suspense**

### **Highland Springs**

Murder Live
Say Bye to Mommy
To Breathe Again
Highland Springs Murders (all 3 in one)

### **The Pretty Must Die Series**

Ripped in Red, book 1
Pierced in Pink, book 2
Wounded in White, book 3
Worthy, The Complete Story

### **Lisa Paxton Mystery Series**

Eenie Meenie Miny Mo
Jack Be Nimble
Hickory Dickory Dock
Boxed Set

Hearts of Courage
A Heart of Valor
The Game
Suspicious Minds
After the Storm
Local Betrayal
Hearts of Courage Boxed Set